9-11
2.0

Fool Me Once…

Richard Lake

$\overline{\text{Lp}}$

Lake Publishing

At no point, will the reader see any reference to the Taliban, Al-
Qaida, ISIS or any other conjured-up enemy of the state. Previous
atrocities committed by so-called religious zealots, have no place
in this work of fiction. The character's names are contrived by the
author. Any reference to any persons living, or dead, is purely
coincidental. All conversation between the characters concerning
the status-quo are real, as are the events and statistics quoted
about modern society. The stated goal of this work is to entertain
and enlighten.

It remains for the reader to discover who the real enemy is!

Cover art by Bony Grafi. Cover design by Marie White.
Edited by S.C.
Book Layout © 2018 BookDesignTemplates.com

9-11 2.0 / Richard Lake. -- 1st ed.
ISBN 978-0-692-06579-2

This book is dedicated to the people of the
United States of America.

Rise like lions after slumber
In unvanquishable number!

Shake your chains to earth, like dew
Which in sleep had fallen on you-
Ye are many; they are few!

— PERCY BYSSHE SHELLY

I wish to state at the onset my deepest sympathy for all who suffered as a result of the initial 9-11 attack. This includes everyone who lost a loved one on U.S. soil, or the subsequent Mid-East wars; to everybody whose life has been forever altered by that unconscionable event.

It is not this author's intention to exploit the horrors of that fateful day. In presenting this work of fiction, it is more to the point of illustrating a what-could-be scenario, which can only be shunned by the awareness of an enlightened citizenry.

With a salute to the venerable authors Aldous Huxley (Brave New World), George Orwell (1984), and Ray Bradbury (Fahrenheit 451), I draw upon their foresight. This, coupled with events and situations many Americans experience daily, serves as the motivation for this story.

-Richard Lake

Part One

ALS – Leaving home

ONE

The headlights racing toward him told Bob the car was going too fast. As the vehicle passed a distant figure on the side of the deserted rural road, three muzzle flashes could be seen. The Impala sped by, the letters G.G. spray-painted on the side. The convertible top was down, showing three young men laughing in the moonlight.

Bob maneuvered his truck off his client's property, turning toward the shooting victim while driving away from the fleeing Chevy. He stopped and leapt out to help the poor soul bleeding on the ground. He found an unshaven man, late thirties, wearing worn—yet not filthy—clothes, with bullet wounds to his back and shoulder. Clear eyes looked up at him as the man mouthed something inaudible and pointed up the road.

Bob, so focused on helping the man, hadn't noticed the Impala stopping and doing a three-point turn around on the narrow highway. Now closing the half mile with vicious purpose, the vehicle was heading back his way. The man on the ground let out a cry of pain as Bob pushed him off the shoulder and dragged him down into a culvert. The Impala screeched to a halt. The driver threw open the car door and jumped onto the blacktop.

"Give me the gun, Homes! Hurry!"

The passenger tossed a pistol to a big angry man with a tattooed face. Catching it like a pro, he pointed the weapon down the embankment and let out three more shots. Bob held his head down as bullets punched the dirt around him and the wounded man.

"Mutherfucker! I'm out! Quick—homeboy—give me some shells. There's a box under the seat. That truck came out of nowhere. The dude saw my car. He could snitch us out. I got to go make sure I got 'em!"

Hearing this, a couple of thoughts went through Bob's mind. First, the gunman most likely had a six-shot pistol. Probably a revolver, which would take a little time to fully load. Also, this was the only gun they had, or one of his buddies would start firing or throw him another gun. His last thought was if he didn't do something—they were sitting ducks.

Grabbing what might have served as a sturdy hiking stick covered with dirt from the culvert, he scrambled up the embankment. The big man facing the car was caught off guard, turning, as the stick broke over his head. He went down, dropping the gun. The passenger tossed the box of shells toward the horrified teenager in the back. He then jumped in the driver's seat and jammed the gearshift into drive. The box of bullets, not caught by the unprepared youth, bounced off the trunk, spilling on the ground as the car started away. Bob ran a few paces and jammed the remainder of the stick into the steering wheel. The car, still accelerating, plowed across the opposite shoulder into a tree.

Looking back, Bob saw his tattooed opponent rub his head still dazed. The man looked around and slowly started to get up. Bob scooped up two live rounds off the street and dove for the gun. Grabbing it in his right hand, he rolled out of reach of his foe, flipped it open and dropped in the two cartridges. Spinning the chamber, he was on his feet leveling the pistol at the gang member. Now furious, the assailant had produced a long-bladed knife from his waistband and was heading toward him.

"I don't know if the first one is a live round or not. I guess it's a matter of how fast you can move and how fast I can pull the trigger. But you can bet I'll pull it if I have to."

The scumbag looked over at his car smashed into a tree. His partner was slumped over the wheel covered in glass. The horn was blaring. He could see the third member of his crew running like a man on fire toward the forest. He dropped the knife.

*****

The Sheriff called to the scene said there were many interpretations for the meaning of the G.G.s street gang. The Ghetto Gladiators, Green Gangsters, Gruesome Goblins, Gutter Grunts, and others. Simply using the term G.G.s defined a ruthless group of drug-dealing killers. Tonight was gang initiation night when a prospective member must prove his worth to be accepted. This was done in various ways, a sense-less act of cowardly murder being a favorite.

The man Bob rescued had tipped over his shop-ping cart, falling into the dirt as the bullets hit him. Spread out along the shoulder were a small cooler, a one burner stove with fuel and a pan, some dry food items, a bar of soap, and a chrome multi-tool. A few clean folded clothes and a novel by a popular author spilled from a backpack. A roll of toilet paper, a water container, a can of beans and a sleeping bag had rolled down into the culvert. The man collected some of these items after thanking Bob before being driven off in the ambulance. A second team of paramedics assisted a handcuffed, foul-mouthed adolescent with glass stuck in his forehead. In the short conversation Bob had with the homeless man, he could tell he was a regular guy. Someone who Bob might have been happy to work with, or call a friend.

As the tow truck pulled the Impala from the ditch, the gangbanger with tattooed teardrops on his face glared at him from the back of the Sheriff's car. Bob told the Sheriff he would make a complete statement the next day, but right now he just wanted to go home. As he got in his truck and pulled away, he recalled the homeless man he had saved. He realized that his possessions were all necessary survival items, not junk collected by a crazy person, a derelict alcoholic, or a tweaker. He couldn't help but think; There—but for the grace of God—go I.

fter arriving home and telling his wife about the events of the evening drive, Bob picked up an open letter from the table.

"Bastards! They turned us down!" He saw tears welling up in Julie's eyes. Wrapped in a thin shawl, she remained silent in the creaking rocker by the small table while staring at the floor. "Military personnel excluded. What a load of crap! Remember what we learned, that there was a correlation between military personnel and contracting ALS? So what if you never saw combat? Is this the way the U.S. Army treats people willing to fight and die for a country they believe in? It just isn't right."

"I know you've tried everything," Julie said, "We all have to die sometime."

"Yeah, I know, but not like this … this is just plain wrong! First Steven in Nam, then Mother, a basket case with the pills, and the useless doctors. All because her eldest son returned from the jungle in a box draped with an American flag." Bob picked up the cat and began petting it.

"Things are different now," Julie said. "The V.A. is expanding nurses' duties. Having them do more regular M.D. procedures because the V.A. itself is so busy. I heard about eighteen vets per day commit suicide and roughly one fourth of all homeless are vets. The doctors there aren't happy at all."

"Yeah, plenty of money for war, not enough to take care of those who served."

Bob crumpled up the rejection letter from the government-funded study of a promising new medicine. In disgust, he threw it toward the wastebasket. He turned away after seeing it bounce onto the floor. The drug, developed by a major pharmaceutical company, had shown great promise in Europe. Like a miracle it could reduce, or with hope reverse, the effects of ALS, also known as Lou Gehrig's disease—Julie's fatal condition. "Did you get a hold of Brandon? Did you tell him we're coming soon, moving to the Lone Star State?"

Julie sat up a bit, her mood changing to a subdued delight, as she spoke of her only son attending college in Texas. "Oh yes, he feels dreadful about our situation here. We talked about the house, your lack of work, and my condition, but he's glad we'll be closer. He says he and Susan are becoming quite an item. We very well may be celebrating his graduation with a wedding cake."

"It'll be good to see him. I guess my new life as an interstate trucker won't be so bad. You can ride with me. We'll see the country: the freeways and big-city loading docks anyway."

"That's right, darling, we'll be together on the open road long as we can, 'til things get bad for me and traveling gets too tough."

Bob was pacing back and forth in the modest home he shared with his wife. "I just wish there was something we could do, some way to get you into that study. You know, this stinks of a cover up. I'll bet since Uncle Sam is putting up the bucks there is a deal with Big Pharma. They're excluding former military because they'd have to admit they royally screwed up, exposing soldiers to some new form of chemical weapon or something."

With calculated movements, Julie arose from the chair. Her condition was getting worse yet she made it over to her husband and put her arms around his neck. "You just reminded me," she said looking into his troubled eyes. "Brandon says his future fiancée's brother is working on a website. Some kind of live video chat thing where people can express their troubles to each other. The idea is they get it off their chest and feel better. What was the word he used? Oh yeah—catharsis. Like an online therapy for disgruntled souls. Perfect for you, Bob."

"Yeah, I'd be a natural at this point. With the State of California reclassifying our area as a high-risk fire zone, forcing an even bigger loss on us after the real estate bubble burst, I'm ready for some kind of therapy. I'm afraid though; some online complaining won't change the lack of employment around here or help your medical situation. By the way, what is this other letter about? I saw on the return address, it was from that lady you knew as a kid, back in Colorado, right?"

"Yes, it was from Lillian Williams, such a dear sweet lady. She sort of adopted me as a daughter, since she had no children of her own."

"I remember you telling me she had the last place on the dirt road where you grew up."

"She did. Had a few dozen acres behind a fence so overgrown with bushes that if you didn't know it was there you would never find it. I used to play in the creek. There was even a spot you could swim in the summer and catch fish all year long. Lillian used to grow most all her own food. She had chickens and a cow, rarely went to town for anything. Lived pretty self-sufficient, really."

"Sounds great," said Bob.

Bob pushed aside a few wild strands of her straight blonde hair while locking on her penetrating gaze as he leaned in and kissed his wife. This was followed by a long hug. He wondered what he would do without her. Once again it seemed the forces of the universe had conspired to shatter his world beyond his control or influence. If only there was something he could do. Something to save his wife, their life, something?

THREE

Julie was a California girl born outside of Denver, Colorado. Her parents moved to the Golden State when she was a teenager. She had a slight sprinkle of freckles, long strands of blonde hair, and wry smile. She was an easy candidate for the cover of an outdoor-sporting magazine. Julie never wore makeup. She couldn't understand why women pasted animal by-products and chemicals you couldn't pronounce all over their faces. She was a nature girl, in her late thirties. She'd met Bob twenty years ago, at a bungee-jumping accident on a bridge along the Colorado River, bordering California and Arizona. She was being rigged up to jump while Bob and some friends slowed to watch—on their way to the Grand Canyon.

Butch, her companion at the time, had not adjusted the tension in the lines after his little brother, Ronnie, made the first jump.

Bob slowed the van. "Check it out you guys. She's jumping—oh my God! Did you see that? She hit her head on that log. It floated down just as she reached the lowest point. They should have checked upstream for that."

"Holy Christ," said Donald, riding in the passenger seat. "She's not moving. Just bouncing limp. It looks like she's knocked out cold."

For a moment, Bob and the others stared in shock at the inert woman suspended from the bridge. Then, Bob jumped into action. He yelled to those on the center of the span that he was going down to do what he could to assist the helpless young lady. Julie was unconscious and could not release herself from her bonds. He shouted up at her companions on the bridge to swing her over to a small section of sandy beach. Soon Butch had attained the necessary amount of sway to swing her within his grasp. Bob was looking up at Butch and the others as he saw young Ronnie loosen the elastic cordage on the guardrail. Being now in a receptive position, Bob was moving his head slightly up and down in sync with the motion of Julie's body, swinging to and fro. He nodded and yelled, "OKAY!" Ronnie released the line, and Bob's future wife landed in his arms, out of the clear blue sky.

"Christ! What happened?" He was lowering her to the ground as she came to. "Who are you?" She was still in a daze, as she reached for her head and felt the painful bash on her skull. The blood on her hand explained the blood on Bob's shoulder. He was now busy undoing the bungee strap around her ankles.

"Bob, my name's Bob. Are you all right? Looks like you've got a little bump on the head. Here, let me see. You should be okay." It didn't seem severe, however there was blood now pouring down the side of Julie's face. "Head wounds tend to bleed a lot. It's so they don't get infected, or get any bacteria, etcetera, in your brain." Bob removed his shirt and proceeded to wipe the blood from her face and scalp.

"Are you a doctor or something?" Julie was studying his well-honed physique.

"Eagle Scout. But we had to practice first aid merit badge on rubber dummies, not pretty girls, like you."

"Well, as long as you passed the class." With their gazes locked, cupid let the first arrow fly. "Man, what do I say? How can I thank you? You saved my life! Hey, I'll tell you what, we've got a campsite a couple of miles down the river. I've got a great wilderness stew, made most of it at home, just have to put it all together really, and heat it up. Plenty of beer, too. Hey, speaking of beer, my fricken so-called boyfriend owes me one—what a loser—almost got me killed. I've had it, that's the last straw. Besides, you'll have to check my bandage later—won't you?"

Cupid's second arrow found its mark as well. "We're supposed to meet some friends along the western rim of the Grand Canyon tonight," Bob replied. "Gunna hike down into the canyon tomorrow. Oh, what the hey. Smitty will wait, doesn't know which trail to take anyway.

"You say you've got some good stew, huh? All my guys know how to serve up is hot dogs and beans. Yeah, I guess we can do it." Standing up and nodding his head with a smile, Bob accepted her invitation. There was something about this girl. "Hey, what's your name anyway?"

She reached out her hand for her newfound hero to pull her to her feet. She responded warmly, looking into his eyes while returning the smile. "Julie."

*****

Uncomfortable as it was, Bob enjoyed their first shared meal. The hot stew was a welcome change from the quickie campfire grub he endured in the backwoods with his buddies. There was something very satisfying about having a decent hot meal, in the middle of nowhere.

Bob noticed how Julie's tatted-out boyfriend, Butch, wasn't much of a camper. She had to tell him to get the wood for the fire from up the hillside, not down by the riverbank. It was easier, and made more sense to bring dry materials down from above, than potentially wet logs up from below. Butch was crude. He spent a lot of time with his skinny little brother talking about rap stars.

Bob considered rap as bad poetry delivered in un-melodic, overbearing, and annoying fashion. Where were the instruments? Where were the harmonies? Knowing their obvious lack of musicianship, those involved referred to themselves as recording artists. Bob didn't hold out much hope for this new style. No, it was rock 'n' roll for Bob, all the way. He was de-lighted to find he and Julie liked many of the same bands. Even though she was two years his junior, they had seen many of the same groups perform on stage. It seemed Julie was a fifth wheel on this quickly planned bungee-jumping weekend. A kind of an odd-woman-out. Butch and Ronnie carrying on, engrossed in their urban obsession, were oblivious to the two seasoned campers chatting calmly by the fire.

*****

Bob had almost forgotten about his three buddies when the camp host arrived to collect the overnight fee.

"How y'all doin'?" said the older gentleman, wheeling up in the modified golf cart.

"Hey Pops. What, you wantin' money again?" Butch responded, agitated at the distraction.

"That's right! You stay for two nights, you pay for two nights."

"What a rip. Damn outhouse stinks, and there weren't no paper this morning when I had to take a crap," Butch said, spilling beer on himself as he took a swig.

"Punks must have stolen it again, or thrown it down the hole," the camp host replied. He lowered his head and with narrowed eyes fixed his gaze on the city boy now stumbling to his car.

Looking over his shoulder, Butch said, "Yeah well, little Julie there had a mishap down by the river so we had to stay another night."

"Oh, a mishap?" The tone in the old man's voice was calculated, questioning.

"Yeah, got bopped on the head, could've drowned maybe." Butch let out a subdued chuckle. "That guy there pulled her in."

"Really, is she alright?" The old man turned his attention to the couple by the fire.

"I'm fine," Julie answered. "A white knight showed up just in time."

"Here's your money, Pops," Butch scowled, having returned from his car, as he extended a couple of crinkled bank notes in the host's direction. He was looking at the girl he had come with and her new-found friend as he stated, "Keep the change, we'll be gone in the morning." Butch turned and went back to the car where the rap music poisoned the tranquil setting.

Bob and Julie gave a parting wave to the camp host as he flopped into his cart, returned the gesture, and headed to the next campsite.

*****

Putting another log on the fire and tossing his head in the direction of the two brothers, Bob said, "What's his deal anyway?"

Julie was moving her chair closer to his while squinting and waving the smoke away from her eyes. "I don't know. He fixed my car. I guess I had a bad battery. We live in the same apartment complex. He changed it and asked me out. He's not really my type, but I agreed. We went for pizza and then to a club. We had another date after that and went back to his place. I wasn't really, how do you call it, 'in the mood' but you know . . . I ended up staying the night. He can be a nice guy, but when he drinks he's a real jerk—like tonight. I needed to get out of the city for a while, chill out you know, so when he invited me down here I said okay. When we get back to Sac I'm going to tell him it's all over, even though nothing's really been started anyway."

"Sac? You mean Sacramento?" There was a tone of excitement in Bob's voice.

"Yeah, Sacramento, California, that's where I live." Julie saw him looking her over, a pleased expression on his face.

"I'm just outside of Chico myself. It's pretty close. Hang on a second, I'll be right back." It didn't take Bob long to walk the short distance to his van and return with a scrap of paper, his phone number inscribed on one side. He handed it to her along with a matchbook and a pen. She took the items from his hand. There seemed to be a kind of magic in the firelight. She dutifully wrote down her own number, and handed the items back.

"Cool," he said. "Well, I better get over to my own camp and crash out. Smitty won't believe this, but he'll be bent if we don't show up pretty early tomorrow. Hell, I didn't even set up my tent, but it was worth it. By the way, your stew was great."

"Hey, you didn't check my wound, doctor!"

"You'll be alright. It's not deep, just clean it really well again when you get home. Put on more antibacterial cream, and keep your eye on it. I don't think you need stitches, or I'd have already said so . . . Good night, Julie." There was a protracted pause. "I'll call you in a few days, see how you are." He turned to proceed back to his own camp but couldn't keep himself from stealing a long gaze at her lovely essence glowing by the fire.

"You sleeping all alone, by yourself, in your tent tonight, are you, doctor?" Her lips conveyed a mischievous smile. The fire popped audibly, and there was a twinkle of knowing in her eyes.

Bob stumbled on an exposed root, his feet no longer under the command of his intellect. "Yeah, I guess so. Looks that way." Fumbling out of sight in the dark, he patted down his nylon jacket. Which pocket is that damn flashlight in? Maybe if I just sneak over later and kill her battery-changing, loser boyfriend—no, strike that, soon to be ex, non-boyfriend. Ah, but then there's also the brother, what was his name? Oh yeah, Ronnie. The fiendish plot flashed across Bob's mind like a late night horror movie on the big screen. He smiled to himself, while the fantasy gave way to reality. Bob knew that he now had to set up his tent by himself, in the dark . . . What a pain.

FOUR

Robert James Revere, in his late thirties, had wavy brown hair and eyes that could convey a serious intent. He was above average in height, looks, intelligence and loyalty to his friends and family. The needle registered at the lower end of the scale regarding his bank account, patience, tolerance for useless regulations, and the stupidity of others. By most accounts he was considered good looking, sporting a style of dress that was casual and comfortable. "Function before fashion," he was heard to say on many occasions.

He was well groomed yet didn't go to any great lengths to impress anybody. On the whole, if you didn't like his appearance he couldn't care less.

Bob was born in the Northern California town of Chico where he attended college. He took basic studies and received an AA degree. During his younger college days he had heard about how the government and the larger corporations were gaining more power and control over the American people; he dismissed this as something he could do nothing about.

Having now matured, he'd become quite disillusioned. Gone were the days of peace and love. Now every day was a struggle to put food on the table, and pay the mortgage on the couple's small house just outside of Ukiah, 80 miles north of San Francisco.

Many regular jobs had been outsourced. Most of the mundane activity done on a computer happened overseas. Falsified government statistics parroted by the lame-stream media to the sheeple counted sub-living-wage, part-time jobs as regular employment. The sheeple, glued to their infotainment propaganda-spewing flat screens were starting to catch on—yet at a glacial pace.

If it had to be done in this country, there was an ever-ready supply of English-as-a-second-language workers. He realized his situation stemmed from the kleptrocracy of the multi-national corporations and their thieving accomplices in Washington D.C. To him the Wall Street Banksters—along with the government—made the mafia crime syndicates look like choirboys.

*****

This was just one of Bob's conflicts. He had to intellectualize himself out of being an angry, depressed person. The little devil on one shoulder was in constant battle with the little angel on the other. The long spear and shepherd's hook often tangled in the deep recesses of his mind.

Bob was in the construction trades. These days you had national hardware and lumber retailers catering to the intruders in their own language. He didn't get his General Contractor's License years ago just to be low-balled by invading hombres having scored some rusty tools at a roadside garage sale. And why, suddenly, did everybody have to adapt to Jalapeno this, and Jalapeno that? Everything from cheese, bread and chips, pizza, to popcorn—even beer—now came with this contrived flavoring. To Bob, it was easy to imagine how the Native American Indians must have felt. History repeats itself. What goes around comes around. It had gotten so bad that people who had known him for years to be honest, reasonably priced, skilled and efficient hired others because they were cheaper, even though they knew he was hurting.

He felt one thing for sure; the fix was in. The purported leaders of his country had merely paid lip service to the idea of border control for decades. He knew there were other national boundaries fundamentally impervious to penetration. The corp-rat CEOs of the United States needed cheap labor to ensure their million-dollar bonuses. They had plenty of financial incentive to encourage cheap workers from foreign lands to dislodge those born on American soil. Undocumented immigrants were unlikely to object to harsh working conditions, or attempt to unionize, for fear of deportation.

In all truth, Bob couldn't deny he'd jump a border fence himself in order to feed his family. He acknowledged the Mexican people were hard workers fleeing a corrupt narco-state with less than five dollars per day as a minimum wage. However, with the U.S. corporations buying off Con-gress, the opposite of pro-gress, Bob was drowning in a tidal wave of foreign worker competition. The salsa-spiced surf was encroaching further up the beachhead every year. The America where Bob grew up was now in a lifeboat swirling in the polluted wake of a deluxe Cabin Cruiser piloted by the ruling one percent. And that lifeboat had a gash in its side.

*****

Before settling into home remodeling, Bob worked a year as a big-rig truck driver. The vocation didn't suit his liking much at the time. Being away from his new wife and infant son was too much for this everyday guy seeking the rewards of simple family life. Truck driving was all right if you didn't object to the isolation, delivery deadlines, sleazy hotels, and lack of sleep. There was not much creative challenge beyond negotiating narrow streets and eye-of-the-needle parking. Once learned, the entire operation, including destinations, was exceedingly repetitive.

Bob enjoyed building houses. Each one was different and it kept his creative juices surging. He wasn't thrilled at the prospect of transporting consumer products all around the southwestern U.S. Although the situation, being what it was, he now looked forward to working for the trucking company outside of Houston. With two semesters left on his son's four-year scholarship, he could rekindle the relationship he had enjoyed with Brandon.

Dodging the bullet of foreclosure, he and Julie sold the home they worked so hard to construct, breaking just about even for the money, sweat and tears invested. Like a shoemaker stumbling about in worn-out moccasins, he might just as well have been a renter all those years, rather than a contractor who toiled to build his own custom home.

FIVE

"You sure you got everything?" Julie was coming out onto the front porch, about to lock the door behind her, as she yelled at Bob. "Not like the last trip to the Sierras where we froze our asses off in the snow?"

"Hey that was a freak storm. Stronger, sooner, and at a lower elevation than expected," Bob responded with a furrowed brow.

"Yeah I remember she was pretty pissed coming back from that one, bro." Rico lit a cigarette after helping load the last of the couple's earthly possessions into the refurbished RV.

"Damn right I was," Julie said. "You're lucky I bought your act at all after that little adventure."

"Relax, lovebuttons, we're going to the southwestern U.S. It'll be in the upper 90's in Arizona, I checked; even hotter in Texas."

"Lovebuttons? That's a new one. Why don't you think up some cutesy names for your buddy Rico, Robert dear?"

"He'll kick my ass. You don't think he got those slash marks in the joint from putting up with cutesy names, do you, sugarbritches?" Bob enjoyed ribbing her but he also knew not to push it too far. They had a long drive ahead of them, and it wouldn't be right to put her in poor spirits.

"Thanks, Rico," was the quiet goodbye as they each gave him a hug. "We'll call you when we get there. I guess from now on you'll have to feed your own cat—sorry. At least I made sure he wasn't locked in the house," Julie said. Bob nodded in affirmation and helped her up into the vehicle.

As he and Julie headed down the dirt driveway, they passed a sign facing the county road connecting the modest five-acre property to the outside world.

No Invitation No Announcement ... No Problem. These three lines were read from top to bottom with the image of a revolver pointed at the reader. "I never did like that sign you made, Bob," Julie commented as they turned south.

"Yeah, I know. I've been pretty bent these last couple of years, with all that's happened, or hasn't happened. It's not really me, you're right. But with street gangs, home invasion desperados, and druggies showing their ugly heads around our former little slice of heaven, it's best to post a strong keep-out message. Doesn't matter anyhow, they've won, we're blowing this locale for some new digs."

"Hey, let's get some of that special sourdough French bread in the city. You know, they say, it can only be made in San Francisco; has to do with a certain enzyme, or spore, in the air. Maybe quite a while before we get another chance." Bob wished he could lasso those few preceding words out of the air, and cram them back down his throat, even if it choked him on the spot. He knew they would never be returning, not the both of them. Julie had a tombstone with her name on it waiting somewhere on a bleak horizon outside of Houston, Texas.

"Great idea! We can get some of that good chocolate for Brandon while we're down on the wharf too." Always thinking of others, Julie had not caught the crux of meaning in Bob's statement. "I know he'll like that." She smiled to herself as she settled into her seat for the long drive.

After the disappointing sale of their house in Ukiah, Bob and Julie had purchased a used 38-foot motor home. Bob had done some repairs to the neglected vehicle in preparation for their trip. This would also offer a degree of comfort for them, since it was to be their home upon reaching the Lone Star State. They figured they would sell it once they found permanent lodging, but not knowing how long that would take, they would be sharing close quarters for a while, at least.

The journey would take them south, through Marin County, and across one of the most adored and iconic structures of civil engineering in the modern world. More than 4,000 feet of six-lane highway suspended some 220 feet above the inlet to San Francisco Bay. A brilliant orange, the Golden Gate

Bridge was one of the top ten most recognizable images, and the most photographed manmade structure
on earth. Also, as a survey had revealed, it was the
most beloved bridge of all time.

Traveling south on Highway 101, the twosome
planned to spend the first night in San Francisco.
They would lavish some of their limited savings on
themselves, as a reward for making the intelligent
decision to abandon the strained economy in rural
northern California. Julie handed out the lunch she
made before they left.

Driving unfettered by previous woes, on a clear
day, Bob was getting used to maneuvering the lum-
bering mass of motor vehicle. Passing a long, slow-
moving funeral procession, he piloted the craft into
the center lane. They were just embarking onto the
causeway out of Marin County, and onto the Golden
Gate Bridge, when he started to hear a disturbing
sound.

"Do you hear that?" Bob asked, turning quickly to
Julie.

"Yeah," she answered. "Did something come
loose on the roof or untied from the back?" A rhyth-
mic flop, flop, flop, sound could be heard over the
music playing across the speakers. Bob switched off
the radio with his right hand just as a loud BANG re-
verberated through the cab. The steering wheel jolted
the ham and cheese sandwich out of his left hand as

iced tea from the cup holder splashed over the center console.

"Bob, look out!" Julie shrieked as the RV lunged toward a bus passing on the driver's side. Plastic dishes, cups and other kitchen items flew off the small galley counter as maps, pens, hair barrettes, and other objects flipped down from the dashboard.

For an instant, as a pure reflex, Bob tried to save his lunch. In the following split second, he grabbed the wheel with both hands and gave a mighty tug, over-steering the rig, and almost hit a young couple overtaking them on a motorcycle on the RV's passenger side. Julie gasped in horror, grasping the center console and door armrest, as the chopper driver jerked the bike to the right. He almost hit the metal curb, sending a panicked group of Japanese tourists diving to the walkway.

"Holy Christ! We blew a tire. Left front, I think." As his foot covered the brake pedal out of instinct, Bob knew that being center-span on the bridge there was no place to pull over and make repairs. He applied restrained even pressure to slow the lurching motor home to a controllable speed.

With traffic now slowing around them, and with Julie negotiating a finger-pointing, hand-waving assist through an open window, Bob was able to get into the right hand lane. He limped the disabled hulk across the remaining portion of the bridge. Finding a turnout off the roadway, on the San Francisco side, he and Julie got out to evaluate the damage.

"Looks like someone worked it over with an axe," was Bob's comment upon viewing the left front wheel and what remained of the tire. "I guess all that time this baby sat in the old guy's lot, the tire must've developed a weak spot or something."

"Maybe it got cracked from the sun's UV light. Well, I'm going to clean up inside. I hope the spare's in better shape, Robert dear. I hope the sun's UV doesn't keep our son from meeting his folks, in their funky old RV."

Looking at each other, they both had a brief chuckle at her statement. The smiles faded, turning into an expression of doom averted, as the black limousine leading the funeral procession they passed earlier made its way by the two of them, out of sight, and around a curve in the road.

SEVEN

Upon completion of a good meal and a night of drinking wine and frolicking in the hot tub of their four-star San Francisco hotel, Bob and Julie felt much better. Although her lower legs continued to bother her, Julie could walk, unaided, with some focused persistence. The couple had done plenty of research into the malady called Lou Gehrig's disease. This unforgiving and fatal disorder progressed from the lower extremities up into the torso, arms, hands, and beyond. When it reached the neck, death was certain. This could be forestalled for a while with tubes supplying oxygen and liquid sustenance to the afflicted.

In a cruel twist, a sufferer could feel pain, but eventually lost the use of limbs, the ability to talk, and in due course, breathe. Suffocating lung paralysis being the inevitable result. There were survivors, and a few opted to cheat death by any means via extensive medical assistance. Those enacting this choice had first-rate medical coverage along with the ability to accept living as a prisoner. With their mind unaffected by the disease, they would endure trapped in a crooked tomb of flesh, physically existing as but a slight resemblance of their former self. Julie hoped for the best, yet prepared for the worst.

She stumbled getting into the coach that would take them to see her only son, Brandon. Being a somewhat poor family, he was lucky to have earned a full scholarship at a renowned university.

"You okay, my dearest?"

"Yeah, I'll make it. It just isn't fair. Going on to serve my country after high school, and this is the thanks I get?" Julie was referring to the mystery regarding former military personnel having a higher propensity to develop ALS than the general population.

Bob fired up the RV. "I'll be glad to get out of here after being overcharged by that band of pirates masquerading as a tire shop. That's for damn sure. Anyway, I hope last night's hot tub did you some good. I would think so, anyway." Bob gave her a long look as he slid the motor home into gear and pulled out of the hotel parking lot.

"Yes, it did. You did me some good, too, lover. Rubbing in all the right places."

"Tell me again about the tornado and the brown powder," he asked her as she put on her seat belt.

*****

"After boot camp I was stationed at Fort Bennington, Kansas, just a few miles outside of Leavenworth. We had reports of an approaching tornado but didn't really think it would hit us. Those were the days before satellite tracking. We expected a shipment of supplies. The place was more like a bunch of storage warehouses than an actual fort, but there were armed guards on patrol 24/7. Evidently, the boxcar full of stuff we were supposed to get was de-railed by some guy in a cement truck crossing the tracks. I heard the engineer survived but the truck driver died. Reports later said the guy was drunk.

"Anyway, they had to load the cargo onto trucks to get it to the fort. This delayed the shipment by more than a full day. By the time it arrived, the storm was on us. The wind was blowing something fierce and we were ordered to hunker down. The delivery guy driving the truck got there at night, just before the cyclone hit. Even though he wasn't military, they violated protocol and let him stay with us in the subterranean bunker to ride out the storm."

"Sounds pretty nasty," Bob said, as he guided the RV onto the freeway.

"You're damn right it was nasty! It was hella nasty. The wind was blowing dirt, leaves, and all sorts of loose stuff all around. Turned out to be an F5, the worst. We had a new C.O. from Seattle, he wasn't real hip about twisters. He should have had the delivery guy park the truck away from the buildings, in a special trench made to help vehicles survive cyclones."

Julie shifted uncomfortably in her seat. Bob could tell she was getting wound-up remembering the traumatic event as she continued. "We stayed in all night. No guards outside, the storm did their duty for them. When we got up the place was devastated, stuff strewn all around. The delivery truck, a flat bed, was turned on its side. It had tipped over and one pallet landed on the corner of a World War Two cannon displayed as a tribute to some famous soldier from that war. On the pallet were some big plastic cylinder containers with Hazmat markings on them. A couple had ruptured and we saw this brown dust spewing out all over the place."

"The next day a bunch of guys in white Hazmat suits, with facemasks, gloves, and clipboards, were on the scene. Everybody except a skeleton crew and a couple of guards were given a three-day pass and sent off base. I was one of the ones ordered to stay and help clean up. Anyway, these guys were going around taking samples of dirt and putting it in little jars. The next day, more guys in even heavier space suits were collecting up the cylinders and loading them into some sort of special truck with hermitic seals. Since it was still a little windy we were all ordered to stay inside during the removal operation. The next week I was assigned to another base in Georgia.

"I heard they relocated everybody and shut down Fort Bennington soon afterwards. Nobody I was stationed with ended up at the Georgia base. The Brass had spread everybody out, so we couldn't talk to each other I guess. We were ordered not to speak about the incident due to national security. They said the stuff was top secret and we weren't supposed to know about it. They reminded us how Leavenworth wasn't shut down and we could wind up there if we broke our silence."

"Sounds like a cover-up if you ask me," Bob said. "They had some new form of deadly biological or chemical warfare stuff—bastards."

"I never thought much about it after that," Julie continued. "I did find my enlisted friend Rachael on social media a while ago. She was sick, and getting sicker. After a short time I saw a notice that her account was deleted."

Bob was silent. He looked at his cherished wife as she was staring out the window. Julie reached for a disposable tissue from the paper box on the center console between them. He watched as she wiped a tear from her cheek. They rode on for many miles without a word between them.

EIGHT

There was a festival in Gilroy, the garlic capital of the world. Julie, being health-conscious, wanted to stop and get some items. Maybe some garlic butter or garlic-stuffed olives for Brandon. Bob didn't mind garlic, but he wasn't an olive man.

Peanut butter was Bob's passion. If they had garlic-flavored peanut butter he would have been a customer, but it was too much to hope for. The world wasn't enlightened enough to combine these two crucial flavors. Chocolate and peanut butter—yes! Almond butter—yes. Peanut butter and banana sandwiches, with mayonnaise—yes. But not peanut butter and garlic, maybe he would try mixing some up himself? No, forget it. No sense risking a good dose of peanut butter on some wild experiment . . . but then maybe?

Another reason they'd chosen this route, through the Central Valley, was because Bob wanted to see the ultimate off-road vehicle. Some guy along the way had taken an old pick-up truck with a V-8 engine, removed the axles and wheels, and put military style tracks underneath. He'd taken a truck and turned it into a tank without a turret.

"Now that's a 4x4 if there ever was one," said Bob.

"Yeah, yeah, big toys for little boys."

"Yeah, well check it out. That one's built to crush the competition," he said with a wry smile.

"I get it, Robert dear. But I'm thinking it's more like over-compensation in an off-high-way." They both laughed at her joke. Of all the things he loved about Julie, her wonderful sense of humor was quite near the top of the list. They climbed back into the RV and continued south toward Bakersfield.

*****

"How much further, Bob? I have to use the ladies' room." Julie was stirring on the seat beside him.

"Not long, we're almost to the turnoff. We just stopped in Fresno a while ago. What a pit, did you know it's been the car theft capital of the nation at least twice? Most drunken city in the U.S. three times.

Remember those guys at the off-ramp? I saw them checking you out. Good thing we didn't get carjacked right there. They call the place Detroit-West, massive poverty. I read where the biggest industry in the Central Valley here is welfare and related assistance to the poor. Subsidized housing, subsidized medical and childcare, that sort of thing. The cops wake up homeless people and tell them to move along. Think about it. That makes as much sense as a helicopter dropping a note to a drowning man telling him to get out of the water. Anyway, don't start with that, 'are we there yet?' bit, Jules."

"Hell, that was a hundred miles ago. I remember the sign. And about the homeless—they should help them. It's mainly about lost jobs. They're not all drug addicts and alcoholics. Many are women and children, some abused. You think the city would have unused buildings to put them up in—start cottage industries—something like that. They put prisoners to work in other places. I'm getting tired anyway. What about a hotel room for tonight?"

"I'll tell you what, we'll take a break at a stop-n-rob market to get supplies. We'll get some good beer, vino, or something to go with the barbecued burgers I'll whip up. But I'd rather shrug the hotel and keep going right now. We can stay tonight in Tehachapi. It's the mountain pass we go over on our way to Vegas. It's about another hour out. I'd prefer to save our money for now."

NINE

"Hey Jules, hold this for me would you?" Bob handed Julie his to-go cup of coffee as he fumbled in his pocket for his keys. The couple had foregone breakfast, being still full from the previous evening's meal and anxious to get on the road.

Bob put the visor down and reached over, doing the same for Julie. The sun was peeking just above the eastern mountains. Later that day they would be past Las Vegas and be headed toward Hoover Dam.

*****

"Wow, what a view." Bob slowed down as they crossed the Hoover Dam bypass bridge. Traffic was light and there was nobody behind them. "What are you doing?" Julie had unstrapped her seat belt, was standing up, and was heading for the galley section of the RV.

"Getting the camera, we have to get a picture of this."

"Yeah, okay, but take it easy, we already decided we weren't going to stop and do the whole tourist thing remember?"

"I know, but we've got to get a shot of this. The Hoover Dam with Lake Mead in the background. Very photogenic, my dear."

"Alright, but hurry, I don't want to get busted for stopping on the bridge. They said it was built to ease traffic across the dam, but you know there's another reason. It's also so nobody can park on the dam with a load of TNT and blow the water supply for the southwestern U.S."

"Only you could be so dramatic, Bob."

"Yeah, well it's true."

Driving on, the couple came upon a large billboard of an insurance company with a smiling green reptile, and shining bold print. The cold-blooded creature was extolling the benefits of getting an auto policy with the company. Underneath the sign, Bob spotted a group of desert vultures tearing the flesh from a bloodied coyote carcass.

"Look at that, Jules. Reminds me of how those insurance and medical bastards treated us. Ripping out our flesh as monthly payments, leaving us helpless by the side of the road in the end. What a sight."

"Like I said, sweetheart, only you could be so dramatic." Julie snapped a few photos of the lake, dam and surrounding scenery, as Bob drove on.

TEN

Bob and Julie's 21 year old, tall, muscular son was fair in complexion with light blue eyes and sandy blond hair. Like his father, he had no problem attracting the opposite sex. He preferred to dress in the latest styles even if it involved a pair of $300 sports-star endorsed athletic shoes—which he couldn't afford. He handled his college courses easily enough, while maintaining his status as a proper street-smart dude.

Brandon had a lot going for him, with great potential. He just couldn't seem to get any traction out of the gate on the road to success. As a young man, he shuffled between living with friends here and there, on and off. Truth was, he stayed mostly with his parents. He worked with his dad infrequently since his father struggled to get his own jobs. His dad took smaller jobs these days and worked often by himself. Brandon would work with his father when Bob could plug him in, yet his paternal benefactor often could not afford the help.

He'd had a few low-wage, dead-end, menial jobs of his own but they didn't last. He'd applied with dozens of potential employers "online" with quite minimal results. For the most part, these positions were commission sales or just plain lousy jobs. He had exhausted most all of the contacts he knew through friends and family. He also possessed a so-called "criminal record." Like many his age, he'd picked up a police jacket with a reckless driving charge.

It made sense this might prohibit him from employment as a driver or delivery person. In reality, it prevented him from getting almost any job. Living in the wired-together world, it was easy to check a person's employment, rental, credit, educational, driver's, criminal, and social media history. If you had any dings on your sheet, you were done for. Your resume, sifted by a heartless computer programmed to search for keywords, was deleted, and it went on to the next person. There were simply too many workers in the unemployment cesspool. That's how it was in society under the modern corp-rat structure. He even had to pay once for a background check for a job he never got. He couldn't help but think at the time: what a scam! He could have told them he wasn't squeaky clean, although he was well qualified for the entry-level position.

No, it was quite evident the corporate-controlled jobs only went to those privileged souls who had connections, college degrees, or unblemished records. And the corporations held the overwhelming majority share of jobs in the employment jungle. That, of course, left the mom-n-pop outfits. These were mostly smaller concerns with jobs going to relatives and friends. There were also the civil or government jobs. This bounced him back to the hurdle encountered in the first category: a blemished record. Beyond that, you had joining the military, an option many of his buddies had taken.

This was a choice he never considered. If he didn't die in some useless war for the multi-national corporate empire overseas, his dad would probably kill, or at least disown him anyway, for knuckling under to the Wall Street-backed military-industrial complex. He remembered his father telling him that initially little Georgie-Boy W. Bush and his co-conspirators at the Pentagon had wanted to call the U.S. misadventure in Iraq 'Operation Iraqi Liberation'. The corp-rat warmongers had to come up off that tag line real quick when they realized what the first letters of each word spelled out.

His loving father would help him out most anyway he could. Once Brandon said to him, "Gee Dad, where would I be without you?" With his widely-known twisted sense of off-color humor, Bob had replied: "You'd be a rotting unfertilized human egg cell, crusted in a cheap feminine napkin—buried under tons of putrid garbage—at the bottom of some stench-fouled land fill."

Sometimes Brandon felt he was already there. In his scant twenty-something years on the planet, he had come to the dire conclusion his plight was hopeless. He had landed on the same patch of disparate ground it took his dear old dad nearly four decades to get to by a republic having been sold down the river in the name of corporate profit. In the time before his scholarship was approved, they had both found themselves spiraling down at the end of a wash cycle. He wasn't overly enthusiastic about his future in this so-called economy, or lack of one.

He knew that more than eighty percent of all stock was owned by one percent of the population, and that the people who owned fully half of the world's wealth could all ride on the same bus. When the news reported the economy was going well, that was who they were talking about. He also knew, if forced to take a high-interest student loan, he would be years in paying it back. Upon graduating, and attaining the middle-class distinction of becoming a homeowner, he would plunge himself into lifelong servitude as a wage-slave. Jobs were scant. The banksters had gotten bailed out, not the people. His higher education was his only chance at a rewarding future.

Brandon was lucky to receive a scholarship at an accredited school in College Station, Texas. Having been conditioned by his father to be wary of the U.S. Government, big corporations, and Wall Street, he took political science as his major while minoring in psychology. Sociology, marketing, and advertising were related courses of study.

He met Dylan in Professor Harold S. Crowder's Poli-Sci class. Dylan McKenzie was majoring in computer science with a minor in political studies and statistics. Dylan's well-established Texas family owned interests in oil and land development. Dylan, a handsome young Texan that could charm a viper into submission, was a freethinking radical ready to buck the establishment at any turn. His anti-government ravings were right in line with what Brandon was used to hearing from his father. Brandon and Dylan hit it off right away. Dylan was working on a website he developed called The Anger Express. This splendid creation allowed people to state their dissatisfaction with the status quo to each other, via live web-cam over the internet. Users could also leave a video for others to watch at their leisure. Articles were presented to inspire comment and discussion. The compelling feature being, this was face-to-face in real time, with an option to record your complaint. Dylan figured with a one dollar app on people's cell phones allowing them to rant to each other, he would be an internet tycoon in no time.

"Looks like they're here," Dylan said, as he turned his lanky frame away from the window, speaking to Brandon in the double-wide trailer. Setting down his beer, Brandon rose to greet his parents pulling up in the RV.

Stepping outside, the two college undergraduates were joined by Susan McKenzie. She emerged from the main house with an excited Golden Retriever.

"Well, we made it," Bob said, as he exited the cab.

"Good deal," Brandon said, giving his father a warm handshake and a man-hug.

"Let's get your mother out, son; she's been having a bit more trouble lately. Her condition's been showing itself more on the drive down here. I had to give her a walking assist around the Petrified Forest. Didn't stay long, but it was kind of cool, a bunch of petrified trees laying all around. Your mother made a joke with the ranger. When we got there she said, 'Hey, I thought it was a forest. What happened, did a logger with a petrified axe come and chop down all the trees?' I guess he hadn't heard that one before. She got a chuckle out of him."

"Yeah, okay I get it, oh, this is Dylan, my roommate, and his sister, Susan."

By now the group had made their way around to the passenger side of the motor home. A slight grimace transformed into a wide smile as Julie was assisted by her son out of the vehicle. Following a warm hug and kiss on the cheek, Julie turned to the attractive young lady standing next to the tall dark-haired lad, now conversing with Bob.

"So, you must be Susan? I hear you and Brandon are quite an item." A raised eyebrow further conveyed the slight questioning tone in her voice.

Susan, breaking Julie's gaze, looked down at her feet. "Why, yes, ma'am, we are. I guess you could say that, ma'am, quite an item." She smiled up at Brandon.

"Adorable," Julie exclaimed. "Brandon, she's absolutely precious. I love the accent. And that's your brother, your roommate?" Julie's attention shifted from Susan and Brandon, with a nod toward Dylan.

"That's my big brother." Susan was quick to answer the question. "You'll get to know Dylan soon enough," she said, a wry inflection simmering beneath her prominent Lone Star drawl.

"You can stay right there for now. Over the week-end we'll get you tapped into the septic and water system and run a cable for electric off the breaker box out back." Dylan gestured in the direction of a utility pole behind the double-wide he shared with Brandon.

"You sure?" said Bob. "Won't it be kind of crowded?"

"Crowded? Jeeze man, there ain't no crowded out here. We've got 320 acres. I don't even have to worry about aiming too high when I shoot a varmint, except for that direction, by the highway, almost a mile off. Besides, y'all is family, right?"

"Well, I guess so, now that you mention it. And speaking of family, isn't it proper to offer your poor old mum 'n' dad a drink after their long ride in this Texas heat?"

"You got it, Pops," said Brandon. "Right this way."

*****

The main house of the estate was a welcome transition from bouncing around in the motor home. With dual-pane windows and a powerful A.C., the five of them enjoyed some repose in comfort with a few cold beers.

There were the usual trappings one expected to find in a southwestern residence. A set of lengthy horns were mounted over the gas-log fireplace, a couple of cowboy horse-riding statue lamps sat on antiqued wooden end tables on either side of the leather couch. Family pictures hung on the walls and were freestanding on tabletops.

As Bob came out of the kitchen after fetching another beer, he picked up an 8x10 framed glossy. Portrayed were two people. A youngster with a familiar face was standing with an older, bearded man, who had an arm around the child. The photo captured the duo in front of a large, weathered, shipping container, with a sign stating; EXPLOSIVES, NO SMOKING.

"Is this you, Dylan?" he said, holding the frame while addressing his host.

"Yeah, that's me 'n' Uncle Joe. Hell, that picture's probably fifteen years old. I was just a kid when it was taken."

"The sign says 'explosives'. What's all that about?" Bob took a lingering pull on the long neck bottle in his other hand.

"Uncle Joe, he's a demo guy, takes down those old high-rise hotels in Vegas, office buildings in Dallas, and elsewhere. Hell, he's even done some work in Saudi Arabia. Learned his trade in Korea, courtesy of the U.S. Army. You'll meet him later."

Bob's mind flashed on a roadside view he'd witnessed, en-route to his new home. A group of feathered scavengers picking flesh off the bones from the corpse of an ill-fated creature of God, under a fifty-thousand-dollar billboard in the middle of the de-sert.

"He ever do any insurance buildings?"

"Say Bob, pass me that stack of ribs, will ya?"

"You got it, Joe. We've been sitting over there in our place in mouth-watering anticipation for the last hour."

"Well we can't have y'all staying so close without offering up some good old Texas hospitality. Now can we? Dylan says he's got you all hooked up with utilities, huh?"

"Your nephew has been great," Julie cut in. "We couldn't ask for better neighbors. Got the water and sewer set up and we plugged into the power the night after we got here."

"Neighbors, heck, y'all are family, ain't ya?" Susan said with a smile toward Brandon.

"Not yet we ain't," said Brandon. "But it might help if I could get another piece of cornbread."

"Why sure enough," Susan replied while passing the tray. "Oh, you'll need butter too. Here ya go." Dylan was silent as he passed the butter to Brandon for Susan.

"How's the job goin' anyway, Bob? I see you parked your trucker's rig off to the side, out of the way, I appreciate it."

"Been going well. The first week they had me doing local hauls as they refer to them here anyway, three, four, five hundred miles or so. I can see why they call this the great state of Texas, great as in big, but the people here are great too. My boss has been real cool, lets me keep the rig here when it's not needed the next day."

"No sweat, partner. Like Susan said, y'all are family. Maggie, never you mind. You know you'll be getting' the bones after dinner, now go lay down and quit botherin' our guests." Joe threw a look toward the dog's bed as the large hound lowered her head and ambled off to her blanket. Turning back to the people at the table he said, "Or is it family?" Smiles lit up faces as heads nodded in silent agreement.

"So, you went to Vegas last week?" Dylan said.

"Yeah, that's right, in fact I drove along some of the same stretch of highway we did on our ride down here. It's a little different though with a big rig. Makes the 38 foot RV seem like a sedan."

"You see any more dead coyotes being eaten by vultures, Robert dear?" Julie said, as she served herself some more potato salad.

"No, but I did see those huge high tension lines, I think that's what you call them, standing all alone, stretching across the desert. They carry the power from Hoover Dam to the southwestern states, right? Vegas included?"

Dylan, not saying much during the meal, now broke in. "Yeah, that's right. I remember you mentioning them along with the dam first day you arrived. You were looking at a picture of me and Uncle Joe and said something about blowing up insurance buildings."

An abrupt silence fell upon the group as beer bottles, forks, and sauce-dripping barbecued ribs stopped in midair. All eyes turned to Bob.

"Uh, yeah, I remember. I've been meaning to ask you more about that. Well not exactly that, I mean, I was mad. Mad at not being able to do anything for Julie. We've been rejected by Physbon Pharmaceuticals. They're doing research on a new drug, Invigratol. It's been legal in Europe for a couple of years. It shows real promise to help her condition, maybe even cure it. The lousy insurance company won't cover it because it's not FDA approved. In my research I found the huge drug companies, you know, Big Pharma, have a lot of influence with the regulators. They may be donating to the FDA to stall approval because they're in negotiations to buy the French company that holds the patent. If they can get the French patent on Invigratol, they can apply for a U.S. patent. I read that the drug may have great potential as a sustainable weight loss application, in an off-label use."

Susan was the first to speak. "Off-label use?"

"Yeah, that's when a drug is good for more than one thing. There is a well-known prescription drug for, how should I say it? Helping men, with, you know . . . men having trouble pleasing their ladies. It was developed for something entirely different than what it's known for." Bob, addressing the group in general, now glanced toward the senior gentleman at the head of the table.

"Humph, well I wouldn't know anything about that," Joe McKenzie countered. "The old pump's still churnin' away, just haven't found a proper well to set it up for since the Mrs. passed on." The diners exchanged glances and broke out in subdued laughter, relieved at the humorous remark.

"Anyway, you know what I mean," Bob continued. "It doesn't seem right. Especially since we discovered it very well may have been her exposure to something in the army. Some odd brown powder, very mysterious. Yeah, I was mad. I still am. Mad at all of them, the insurance company, the drug company, the U.S. government, both the army and the FDA. I guess Physbon Pharmaceuticals doesn't have enough millions of dollars stacked up in their Chicago office. They have to let some people die, so they can rack up more billions later on. When I saw the picture of the sign for explosives, something in me wanted to blow the crap out of all of them. Blow them all to hell. Maybe those high-tension lines in the desert, from Hoover Dam to Vegas. Do something, it's my wife." Now turning to Brandon he said, "Your mother, she's dying, and it's because of them. A lion doesn't kill a thousand goats, keeping them for himself, while his clan starves. The Aborigines consider greed like we're subjected to by big-pharma a form of mental illness."

A solemn mood settled over the table. Susan stole a look at Brandon, then at Dylan. Joe McKenzie pushed his creamed corn around on his plate in silence. Dylan looked at Bob and took a long pull on his bottle of beer. Julie was the first to speak.

"Really Bob? That's a nice thought, I think, but you just can't go around blowing things up because you're mad at the world. I understand, and I appreciate it, but really. Even if you could do it, it wouldn't be right. People would be killed, innocent people, no, it wouldn't be right."

"Oh I don't know, we've blown a lot of stuff up and nobody got killed," Dylan chimed in, now glancing at Demo Joe, "Haven't we, uncle?"

"Sure have, been doing it for years, lots of fun too," the elder member of the clan smiled.

It was Brandon who weighed in next. "Yeah, but then we'd be terrorists, wouldn't we?"

Dylan answered, "Hey, do you remember what Professor Crowder said in Poli-Sci class first semester? The trouble with terrorists is they kill a bunch of people and then everybody hates them. A lot of so-called terrorists just want to make a statement, but they go overboard by demolishing a nightclub or a train station. Then nobody cares about why they did it in the first place."

"Yeah, it's terrible. I guess that's why they call them terrorists." Susan blushed in embarrassment at her obvious statement. The others looked at her and grinned, and then she said, "What about some pecan pie, y'all ready for some dessert?" She gathered some empty plates from the table and glided off to the kitchen.

"You know, before they called them terrorists like now, back in my day they were called activists," said Joe.

"That's right," Bob interjected, "Now some disgruntled ex-employee picks up a rifle and takes out some people at the local shopping mall and they call him a terrorist. Really, he's just some guy who's pissed off and doesn't know what to do. I know the feeling. He's not a terrorist. A terrorist has an agenda. We got caught in the so-called economic downturn. That's why we're here. Had to start over. But the term terrorist is way over-hyped. Used to justify wars in the Middle East. Before there were terrorists there were commies." Bob raised his beer and gave it a tilt toward Joe. "Remember that?"

Joe picked up his glass, made the same gesture toward Bob and took a sip. "I remember," he replied with a nod.

"Recovery. They talk about economic recovery. What a joke. I remember growing up, there were bums. I'm sure there always have been. But now we have an entire class of people called homeless. When I was young you would have to think for a minute what that means, homeless. Not anymore, now the word is in common usage."

Susan entered and set down a golden, steaming pie. In the other hand, she gave her brother some plates. "Dylan, pass these around will you please? I'll be right back with some silverware."

Breaking a thoughtful look on his face, Dylan took a plate for himself and handed the stack to Bob, as he said, "What if you could use the power of a terrorist action, without killing anybody, and get the same results? Say by doing something really slick, something no one else has thought of?"

Bob receiving the plates gave him a long look, searching his eyes before responding, "Yeah, what if you could? What if you could actually make a difference?"

Dylan shot a glance at Brandon, who was observing the two of them across the table with piqued interest. Before taking a long slug finishing his beer, he repeated, "Yeah, that's an idea, what if you could do something really slick?"

Part Two

The Plan – Things That Go Boom

"Watch yourself, the last step is loose. Is Brandon coming out?" Dylan said as he walked into the late afternoon Texas heat and lit up a cigarette.

"Yeah, I think so," was Bob's reply. "I think he's helping Susan with clearing the table. She seems like a great gal, I'm happy for him, and for all you've done for us. Your family has been very kind, Dylan."

"Hey, I brought out an after-dinner beer for us," Brandon said, descending the stairs.

"Why thank you, son." Taking two of the open long necks, he handed one to his host. "Say, mind if I get one of those from you?" Bob gestured to Dylan's lit cigarette.

"What's that, Dad? You don't smoke."

"Well you're right, not for twenty-two years, or so. I quit right around the time you were born. I'm just uptight about your mother, the new job, our situation, you know."

"It'll be okay, Dad, somehow, I'm sure of it." He turned to his friend and future brother-in-law, "Say, Dylan, what was it you were saying in there about doing something slick? Something no one else had done before."

"Well, I had an idea. You know what potential energy is right? When something has the power to do an action, but is currently in idle mode, disconnected?"

"Yeah, I guess. You mean like a big rock on a high ledge that could fall if disturbed?"

"That's right. And I like your use of the word disturbed, we could use that."

"What do you mean?"

"Like we were saying at dinner, real terrorists go around shooting and blowing stuff up. Then everybody hates them for it, right? Well, what if someone did acts of, I don't know what you would call it, pseudo-terrorism, light terrorism, simulated activism." Dylan took a long pull on his beer; Bob and Brandon, following his prompt, did the same.

It was Bob who spoke. "Alright, like Brandon said, what do you mean?"

"What if we took some of our cases of dynamite, just the empty boxes, and placed them around the footings of a couple of those high-tension line towers in the desert you were talking about. We then take a picture, maybe with a sign showing Las Vegas 20 miles, and send it to the government with our demands? Actually, scratch that, we superimpose a big question mark over the picture and state a request to have some governmental policies overturned?"

"What's that supposed to do?" Brandon asked.

"We shame them into a policy reversal."

"That's crazy," said Brandon. "Illegal as hell too."

"Hey, it's illegal what they're doing to this country. Not to mention all the undeclared wars in foreign lands. We're practically in a fascist state now. Big Pharma, Big Oil, Big Tele-com, all mobbed up with the government. Isn't it illegal what happened to your mom? First they made her sick, and now they won't even take care of her. To me, that's pretty illegal, don't you think?"

Bob had been listening without interruption until now. "But how is that going to work? I mean, if we don't actually blow anything up, won't they think it's just a prank or something?"

Dylan locked on his gaze. "We shame them into meeting our demands. You know that 12-pack of beer we opened before dinner? If you saw only the carton, you would know the real beer had to be around somewhere, right? Well, it would be the same with an empty box of explosives. Hasn't Brandon told you about our website? The Anger Express? It's a real-time chat room for angry people. You log on, and can express your dissatisfaction with the status quo via two-way live video. You can also leave a video of your grievances to be reviewed later and commented on by others. You've heard of instant karma? This is instant, two-way, live catharsis. You get your frustrations out, so you don't have to kick the cat, hit the wife, or go postal with an AK-47."

"Julie mentioned you had some sort of social venting internet thing going, but I didn't know just what it was. Sounds good. People need an outlet for anger, I know I sure do," Bob said.

"That's right," Dylan continued, "there is no socially acceptable outlet for anger in our culture. Sure, some people drink too much," a wry grin crossed his face. "Some people take it out at the gym, or punching bag. Some keep it inside, where it festers like a tropical wound only to come out later with a gangrenous vengeance. The Anger Express allows a person to get it off their chest and not get fired, divorced, or pull down a lengthy prison sentence."

"It's a cool deal, Dad. Dylan and Professor Crowder came up with it. It's up and running. We already have a few thousand regulars and our unique visitors are increasing all the time."

"Unique visitors?" Bob raised his bottle for a sip of beer, only to find it was now empty.

"That's right, that's how we monitor the website's popularity. The more unique visitors, or new customers you have, means your website is catching on."

"Alright I get it," said his father, "but what are we gunna do? Say we load some boxes of C-4, TNT, or what-have-you under the towers and take a picture with a big question mark over it? Are we then going to ask Physbon Pharmaceuticals or the FDA to release this medication for your mom? That would be a major bust, wouldn't it?"

"We don't do it so obviously. There are many things wrong with this country. We can conceal our demands, leave a false trail. We demand they reverse the Supreme Court ruling called Citizens United. That little piece of underhanded legislation gave huge multi-national corporations the power of unlimited campaign donations. Essentially it granted them cart-blanche to support, or buy, any candidate they choose."

"Yes, I've heard of that." Bob was now looking for somewhere to set down his empty bottle.

"Also the Patriot Act," Dylan continued. "Now there's a doozy! Passed in the middle of the night while most of Congress was on vacation. They fundamentally shredded The Constitution with that one. It allows unwarranted search and seizure, also indefinite holding of anyone. Did you know you could be walking down the beach in Monterey, Miami, or Long Island, with a sign reading, 'Save the Whales,' and they can construe it as an act of unruly defiance, or to use the more common term—an act of terrorism. That's what the military prison in Guantanamo Bay,

Cuba, is all about. People being held, and not charged with a crime, for as long as the government wants."

"It'll make them think," Bob said as he threw down his cigarette and ground it out with his shoe.

"Hey," said Dylan, as he reached down and picked up the butt while flicking the last burning ember from his own smoke. "If it's made by God, it stays in the sod. If it's made by man, it goes in the can." The others watched as he put both butts in his empty beer bottle.

Bob now handed his bottle to Brandon while throwing a glance toward the front door. Brandon got the hint. "Okay," he said, "I'll be right back."

"Wow." There was exasperation in Bob's voice. "I've been so wrapped up in my own problems. I didn't know it was so bad! That's regular police-state action if you ask me."

"Now you're catching on," Dylan continued. So what we do is we muddy the waters with these demands for change, while including a statement regarding the over-regulation by the FDA of certain substances or procedures that should be more readily available. Naturally, the quick approval of Invigratol is included. We post the video, anonymously of course, on the website."

"Yeah," Bob interjected. "As soon as I found in my research that Physbon Pharmaceutical's Invigratol, Julie's lifesaving medicine, can be used against the epidemic of obesity in this country, I knew it was a gold, diamond, and platinum mine, all rolled into one for those god-damned greedy bastards."

"I get it," said Dylan. "So what we do is something like those murder stories you see on TV. If you want to kill one guy, you do it, and then kill two or three more, to throw the cops off track."

"I like it," said Bob. "But we can't let Brandon's mother catch wind of this. There's no way she would approve, even if it would save her life. She's just too good a person to get wrapped up in something like you're suggesting."

Brandon, having returned a moment ago with a fresh round of cold beers, acknowledged his father's concern. "Yeah, Dad, I hear ya. If we do something like this, we have to keep it on the DL from Mom."

"The DL?" Bob twisted off his bottle cap.

"The down low," Dylan clarified. "You want to take a look at the supply shack, the modified storage shed, where we keep the stuff that goes boom? Give me a minute, I'll get the ATV, it seats four. The shack is down the road apiece. We keep it away from the house and double-wide for obvious reasons." Dylan turned and was already on his way to the small garage, next to the regular garage by the house.

"Yeah, sure." Glancing at his son who was now looking a bit troubled, Bob said, "You coming?"

Without answering, Brandon followed his father toward the corner of the house. He walked in silence for a few paces before inquiring, "Hey, aren't we gunna need a couple more beers for the ride?"

Bob, looking back, smiled at his son. "Let's check out the goodies first, we'll worry about that when we get back."

FOURTEEN

Dylan wasn't kidding about having an abundance of impressive stock in his uncle's steel storage shack. Just as any contractor would accumulate leftover materials from a lifetime of building homes and other structures, old Demo Joe had more than his share of leftovers from a decade's long career of bringing buildings down. Inside the converted Sea-Train container with adjoining metal paneled shed was an assortment of half-full boxes of dynamite, some canisters with the well-marked word Nitroglycerin in bright red letters on the side, some orange plastic wrapped elongated 'salamis' of a play-dough looking substance, some old plunger type charge detonators, kegs of black powder, a mixture of blasting caps, coils of fuse, multicolored wire, and shaped charges.

There was also a lot of stuff Bob could only identify as being timers, and other assorted electronic detonators and components. In addition, there were many empty or almost empty boxes of most all of these materials. Evidently, Joe wasn't much of a neat freak when it came to organizing his storage area. Bob knew things could be removed without being noticed for some time, if ever.

After viewing the items in the shed, Dylan exclaimed with a grin, "You know what they say—a man is only as good as his stash." He continued, "So, Bob, when's your next trip to Vegas?"

"In couple of weeks. It's a regular route, along with others I'll be going to. They send me to different states all around the southwestern U.S."

"Okay, we put our plan into effect on that delivery."

"Are you really going to do this, Dad?"

"I guess so. We've tried the mister nice guy approach and burned through all of our appeals at this point. You don't have to be involved if you don't want to be, son. It's not your fight."

"Like hell, she's my mom. A person only gets one mom you know!"

"Yeah, I know, but we'll have to be cool about it. We can't all be trucking off to Vegas and have your mom seeing something on the evening news about a wild band of misfits trying to blow up electrical towers with empty boxes."

They couldn't help themselves at this point; the trio broke into a fit of laughter at the mention of the bizarre action the group was contemplating. The way Bob had said it, it all seemed quite insane.

Dylan, making waving hand gestures in the air, brought the men back to reality. "Alright, listen, we'll have to keep the womenfolk in the dark, that's for sure. I've got a buddy down at the gulf who runs a charter service. We'll say we're going fishing for a few days, out 150 miles or so, and staying overnight on the boat. Instead, we'll be riding with you to do the dirty deed in the desert. I can even have my friend ship up some fresh fish so it looks like we caught something."

Bob, giving Dylan a discerning look, said, "It looks like you've put some thought into this. You vying to be some sort of super criminal or something?" His mind jumped to a scene in a movie. In the scene, the movie's master criminal is conducting a meeting with other international crime bosses. He makes the statement how man has gone to the moon, split the atom, and done other incredible achievements of all sorts—except crime.

"Hey, they've weaponized the news against us—only showing us what they want us to know. Hell, the world news starts off with a national weather report, goes into an array of local murder or human-interest stories, and ends with video of the president's dog, or some other useless subject. The daily news is designed to sell you something. The media is the fourth arm of government. They're the mouthpiece for the deep state, the globalists. They propagate stories about politicians engaged in immoral sex or bribery, so that when they bring them down they'll have public support. They tell you almost nothing about what's really happening in the world. We won't be carrying protest signs; we'll be carrying out for-real signs of protest."

Brandon felt a vibration in his pocket; he pulled out his cell phone. "Hi Mom." There was a pause while he listened. "Yeah, we're heading back there now. Dylan's just showing us some of the grounds, got some cool old stuff out here on the back forty." After another short pause, "Love you too." He returned the device to his pocket before saying, "Okay, I guess I'm in, but I hate lying to Mom."

With a look of pride on his face, Bob answered, "I know, son, but right now your mother has no chance, no hope, nothing. And when you're in a place of nothing, you've got nothing to lose."

FIFTEEN

Two weeks later, Bob picked up his newly acquired partners-in-crime at a pre-arranged location, just off the interstate. After loading some paper wrapped boxes, three stuffed utility bags, and a couple of personal travel satchels in the trailer of the big rig, Brandon climbed in. He seated himself in the rear of the cab, or sleeping compartment, of the semi-tractor. Dylan slid into the passenger position.

"So let me get this straight," said Bob, pulling onto the highway while shifting gears. "We stack a bunch of your empty dynamite boxes around the high tension towers coming out of Hoover Dam. We take pictures of them, indicating they lead to Vegas with a big question mark ghosted over the photo. We send it to the Feds, along with a list of demands for change and we hope we don't get caught in the process. Then we sit back and wait for this massive transformation of reality?"

"Something like that. Most likely it'll take more than one event to enact any real change." Dylan was checking out all the accessories on the instrument panel as he spoke.

"Somehow I knew you were going to say that." With clutch applied, another gear was enmeshed.

"How're you going to send this out and post this on your website anyway? Seems like that'll lead them right to our—I mean your—doorstep."

"What I'll do is enter it, encrypted, through a proxy server, sent from a coffee shop, or some other Wi-Fi hotspot. I've already written proper coding to cover our tracks. I've given the message pinball marching orders. It'll bounce off dozens of servers around the globe before showing up at the Supreme Court, the Halls of Congress, a few Big Pharma types, the FDA, and, of course, the president."

"Holy Christ!" Brandon was leaning forward from the back of the cab. "You're, I mean we're, emailing the president? I guess I never thought about that."

"Hey, I'm in the shotgun position here, so I say we use the shotgun approach. SOB's simply a temporary employee to give the people the illusion they have some say in governmental policy. Besides, he's going to hear about it anyway. So it might as well be from us."

Bob let this last bit roll around in his mind before responding. "If we're going to remain anonymous, you know, not end up in a hole lit with striped sunlight, who are we going to say this little request is from?"

"Well, remember the other night, bro," Dylan said, leaning toward the third member of the team. "Remember when I was up late at the computer?"

"Yeah, I remember, I couldn't sleep either."

"I was working on a name for our little troop of conspirators."

"Okay, what'd you come up with?"

"Check it out, it's perfect—The Pacific Tribal Rioters."

Bob now shot a glance at Brandon, seated in the back, then Dylan, to his right. "What, the Pacific Tribal Rioters? What kind of a name is that? Besides we're out of Texas now, aren't we?"

"That's correct. But originally you guys came from northern California, right?

"Yeah, so?"

"So it pays homage to that little fact. Plus by doing so, the blue meanies will be looking in that neck of the woods, not down our way. But that's not the best part."

Bob turned up the A.C. before asking. "Okay, I'll bite, what's the best part?"

"The best part is what it really means. You can extract letters from the name in proper order to spell out the word, PATRIOTS."

Bob and Brandon were still for a moment before both, speaking in almost perfect sync, said, "You're right." Brandon continued with, "That's brilliant, Dylan."

Bob turned to the others with a smile now gracing what had been a strained look on his face. "I like it. You know, this little escapade reminds me of something I heard a long time ago. Tickling the Dragon's tail. I guess that's what we'll be doing, huh?"

"Tickling the Dragon's tail . . . " Dylan grinned as he spoke. "We're gunna torch up a metaphorical bonfire under that mythological mutherfucker's bulging ball sack! That's what we're gunna do!"

The trio broke out in unrestrained laughter. Brandon popped the cap on a couple of cold ones from the ice chest beside him before handing them forward. A third pop could be heard from the back of the cabin soon after. Bob turned on the radio. Country wasn't really his first choice, but it seemed more than appropriate at this time.

The crew drove many miles, sipping beers, listening to stories set to music of broken hearts, repossessed trucks, and the affection of long lost dogs, while watching the scenery go by in silence.

SIXTEEN

❝So what did you get? Bob asked.

"Late model Ford, dark color, V8, just in case."

"In case we have to outrun the cops, you mean?"

"You never know. Best to be prepared," Dylan replied.

"How'd you score a rental if we're supposedly doing all this while staying incognito?" Brandon inquired.

"Got a few tricks up my sleeve. For one, I used a stolen credit card matched to a fake I.D. You can buy blocks of them out of Romania from an internet dark site, if you know where to look. Signed for the rental agreement with my left hand also, just in case."

"That trick is so old, Charlemagne could have used it to sign the Magna Carta," said Brandon. "Besides, I thought we were doing victimless, what did you call it? Pseudo-terrorism."

"Yeah well there was a camera on me but I kept my head down, with hat and shades on. Besides, the credit card company will have to pay anyway—you know—the evil banksters not the actual person, so don't sweat your 'nads. At least we got a car so we don't have to park your father's big rig by the road-side, on our way hiking out to the scene of the crime."

"I'm glad you thought of that," said Bob. "Won't there be a GPS transponder in the rental car marking our stopping point along the road? You know, an easy tip-off to the authorities?"

"I'm sure there is," Dylan answered, "but I doubt anyone will be looking unless the car is stolen or not returned in a reasonable time according to the con-tract."

"Hey, how come only two beds?" asked Dylan, scanning the room and stepping inside.

"That's all they had," answered Bob. "Busy time of the year, I guess. Look around, this is no Sultan's Palace, just your basic no-tell motel. Don't worry, I'll sleep in the truck. You guys can have the room. Did you get beer on your way back?"

"Yes I did. Some good stuff too, not the domestic swill you guys are used to."

"We're not made out of money, remember? Let me have one of those," said Bob. "I need to get some liquid courage in me before we set off on this little midnight stroll through the desert. Got a few hours to kill anyhow."

*****

It was after 1:00 A.M. before the three men left their room in Boulder City to drive out to a point along Lakeshore Road off Highway 93. They parked the rental car and hiked to the high-tension towers carrying untold megawatts of power from the great dam to Sin City. Dylan had arranged the backpacks with all the necessary supplies to carry out their little caper. The empty dynamite boxes had been folded neatly and placed in packs along with clear two-inch tape for ease of reassembly. Included were two one-million-candlepower flashlights, some wire, one of the timers from old Demo Joe's supply shack, gloves, and a digital camera. Brandon inquired about one bulky bag making a clanking sound while the trio moved out. "Hey, what's with this one?"

"Climbing gear," was the short answer given by Dylan.

"Climbing gear?"

"That's right, I figure we'll climb up the towers a ways and strap the boxes up there closer to the wires."

"What," said Bob. "Climb the towers in the middle of the night?"

"That's right."

"Whatever for? I thought we were just going to place the boxes around the base and take pictures."

"It'll have better dramatic effect if the pictures show we placed the explosives higher in the towers and closer to the wires. You know, to ensure the lines would be severed. If we only blew the legs off the bottom, the towers themselves could just set down in place. The high voltage lines could stay intact. It'll indicate we're willing to go the extra mile to get the job done right."

They were up over a hill now, out of sight of the road, when they stopped for a short break. "So who's going to climb the towers?" asked Brandon.

Bob and Dylan looked at each other before focusing their gaze on Brandon.

"Oh no," the younger member of the group proclaimed, "not me."

"I concur, it will make for a more convincing photograph," Bob said.

"Yes it will," Dylan agreed. "Good of you to volunteer, dude. Remember, like you said, a person only gets one mother in this life. Don't forget who you're doing this for."

"Yeah, yeah, I remember. Funny how, right about now, I wish I was adopted." Bob shook his head without speaking, as the trio resumed their trek toward the towers.

*****

"You were right about wearing dark clothing. There's more moonlight out here than I would have imagined," Bob stated as they approached the chosen tower. Dylan reached into one of the bags and pulled out a bulky, odd metal object.

"What the hell is that thing?" Bob said as he pulled a pack from his pocket and lit up a cigarette.

"It's a collapsible small boat anchor. See you flare out these flukes, lock in this sliding collar, and you've got an anchor for a small boat. Or a redneck gaff for scaling walls, buildings, or, in our case, the climb-proof metal mesh below the ladder you see up there. Also you better cup that thing. When you take a drag off it, the light can be seen for more than a mile. Especially on a clear night like tonight."

"Wonderful, so I'm doing a Bat Man act on my way scaling up the tower huh?"

"Unless you're wearing shoes with those little wings on them, and as far as I can see, you're not. Bob, why don't you put your gloves on and start preparing those boxes so bat boy here can hoist them up when he gets in position."

With a well-practiced, rodeo round-up swing, Dylan let the gaff fly. It caught a steel framing member above the climb preventative metal mesh at the base of the tower. Brandon, being young, possessed good upper body strength, and now wearing gloves, scrambled his way toward the stars. He climbed an excess of 75 feet up the sturdy electrical structure while trailing a length of climbing rope from his belt.

No lights were used in this process as the group didn't wish to draw attention to themselves on this Wednesday evening out amongst the scorpions, snakes and desert rats. Upon reaching the 'neck' of the structure where the supporting framework splayed out to carry the massive insulators and wires the diameter of a man's arm, he set his perch and began to pull up the empty boxes marked Caution: High Explosive. Brandon strapped three boxes to the framework, making sure the bold crimson markings on the boxes were right side up and readable from the ground. He was feeding in the ends of a pair of twisted red and black detonator fuse wires, connected to a timer, as a low roar approached from Lake Mead.

"Holy shit! Sounds like a chopper!" exclaimed Bob. He was looking at Dylan before turning his concerned gaze into the skeletal monolith looming above. His only son was now trapped in a crow's nest doing what others could only interpret as an act of out-and-out sabotage. "Hold on! Don't move!" yelled Bob above the increasing wap-wap-wap of the rotors.

Brandon looked toward the helicopter, then down in horror as he slipped, dropping a pair of electrical pliers. The chopper made its way a scant 1000 feet above the power lines. As he looked up, Bob could make out the insignia of the Clark County Sheriff on the underbelly.

"Oh my God," said Bob, climbing out from the slumped position he and Dylan had taken behind the nearest concrete pylon. A loud 'clang' sang off a metal truss above him as the pliers bounced off, careening into the sand a few feet away. With a raised voice, "Brandon, are you alright?"

Brandon hung on, hands clinging to the unforgiving steel suspending his life like a featherless baby bird, unable to fly, stuck high in a spindly tree.

"Yeah." The word was inaudible. "YEAH!" Louder, so his ground crew could hear him. "I guess so."

"Looks like they didn't see us . . . Amazing," said Dylan. "Must've been looking farther forward, at the dials, or something. They didn't slow down or turn around."

"Yeah, thank god, let's hurry up and get out of here," was all Bob could answer.

"No doubt." Now, yelling up at his college buddy, Dylan said, "The boxes look good, move the wire and timer so they can be seen from here and come on down."

*****

With the crew assembled at the foot of the tower, Dylan pointed the camera on the explosive cartons strapped high in the metal framework while Bob and Brandon focused the powerful flashlights.

"Hurry up," said Bob. "We're not filming a documentary. Let's get the hell out of here."

"Yeah, I know, but we've only got one shot at this, unless you want to come back tomorrow," Dylan said as he worked the camera.

"Hey, what about the Vegas 20 miles sign?" said Brandon.

"Don't worry about it. I can patch it in later with the big question mark I'll edit over the photo. We do that, along with our list of governmental changes, and our intentions should be clear."

"I hope you're right," said Brandon.

Bob, now sitting on the foundation of the pylon he had ducked behind, took off his gloves and lit another cigarette. "Yeah, I hope you're right."

"Hey remember to cup that thing, and don't throw your butt on the ground."

"A fiberglass filter will return to the elements in 25 years or so, especially when buried in the ground. I learned that from a park ranger many years ago. So I wouldn't worry about littering too much out here in the desert, Dylan. It's not like on the road at your ranch."

Dylan, having completed the photo shoot, was placing the camera in the backpack while Brandon was slinging his over his shoulder. "DNA," he said, while reaching out a hand to help Bob to his feet. "And don't touch that metal without your gloves on—

don't want fingerprints. We're taking 'leave no trace' to the extreme."

Bob retracted his hand from where he was about to grab the metal member to pull himself up, and now offered it to Dylan. "Yeah, I guess you're right. We better take it to the extreme."

SEVENTEEN

"That will be $14.45, sir. Do you have a rewards card?" the checkout associate at the 24-hour drug store asked.

She wore a nametag that read Misty. Bob doubted it was her real name judging by her features. She was chewing gum. He noticed she stopped the disrespectful behavior when a manager-type came to help another customer at the next register. She might have been pretty, if she removed the small silver nose ring, the excessively large earrings, and tattoos showing above her collar. The spiked hair could use a rework as well.

"No," Bob said, and handed her a ten-dollar bill and a five-dollar bill. He kept them in his wallet in a special section. She didn't notice that he deftly handled them between his fingers, never touching them with his fingertips. With his head down, he figured the baseball cap obscured a good image of his face from the camera above. Other cameras, in more distant areas of the store, were pointed at specific aisles and easily pocketable products.

"Would you like to sign up for one and receive our special offers?" she said.

"No thank you, not today." He was careful to speak in a monotone, with no accent or inflection to his words, which he kept to a minimum. Be polite, don't say too much. Give them the very least to subject to any voice print analysis, should one arise. He was practicing his cover. Do your best not to be remembered. Don't make small talk. Don't mention the date or day of the week, so as to not make any unnecessary imprint in the cashier's mind. Be incognito when out in the big bad world. This had been discussed by the men at length on the trip to Nevada.

She punched in the $15. Bob watched as she took the money and checked the display depicting the readout of the transaction. He knew she was looking at the amount of change to give the customer for the amount received. It didn't take a math whiz to figure out the amount was fifty-five cents.

He accepted his change, flashed a curt smile and a nod while looking up only slightly, and said thank you to the girl. He picked up the bottle and left the store before she could put it in a bag. No need for a cheap plastic pouch for an easily toteable single item.

Saving a little ecology one bag at a time, he thought to himself as he left the store.

Bob was of the notion that the sales associate had been bred for the position. Corporate America only wanted people smart enough to punch the buttons on their point-of-sale machines, cook their burgers, deliver their pizzas, and sort and stack cheap Chinese crap on store shelves. He returned to the no-tell motel across the street.

*****

Dylan had written the letter on a standard, older computer. The computer had no phone lines leashing it to 'Big Brother'. There were no wireless connections either from the computer to the 'net, or from the computer to the printer. The letter was simple and to the point:

> To whom it concerns,
>
> The action by the Supreme Court obscenely called Citizens United, that corporations have the same free speech rights as living people, along with the perversely titled, Patriot Act, must be reversed. In addition, all pharmaceuticals, and medical procedures, allowed in other modern countries, must be made available to Americans.

We will be monitoring the national news networks this coming Labor Day.

The broadcast must include a statement that Citizens United has been rescinded. A reasonable limit on campaign donations will be established. Also included must be a statement concerning the reversal of the Patriot Act. Along with this announcement the abolishment of restricting certain medical procedures and beneficial medicinal compounds as currently established by law, will be affirmed. You will assure the public that these medicines will now be covered by insurance under reasonable conditions.

The absence of these statements, on the prescribed date, will result in a display of our conviction upon one of your key interests. It is not our intention to harm our fellow citizens, yet due to the nature of our reprisals—people may die.

THIS WILL BE ON YOU!

Failure as anything less than full compliance with these stipulations will result not only in massive avoidable damage, but we will inform the people of the United States that you were warned—and did nothing.

We will make the public aware their government let this happen. It will be as though you committed the act yourself.

A real group of United Citizens.

Also, any reference to our organization as 'Terrorists,' will be dealt with in a most extreme fashion. We are citizens for political change; we are the:

Pacific Tribal Rioters.

PATRIOTS

*****

Now working on his laptop in the motel, Dylan was superimposing the video taken previously that evening with a large question mark, and a photoshopped rendition of a Las Vegas 20 Miles sign. Bob walked in and set the bottle of tequila on the small table by the bed. "Say, Brandon, take that ice bucket and fill it up, will you? Oh, and grab the coffee mug out of the truck please. I only see two cheesy little plastic cups here in the bathroom."

"Okay, Dad."

As he left the room, Dylan looked at the bottle of tequila. He turned to Bob, and said, "Power-lounging now, are we?"

"Yeah well, after that little escapade earlier, I need to unwind a bit."

"I hear you. This will be ready to upload to the 'net tomorrow. I saw a small coffee shop with a 'free wireless' sign on our way out here. It'll be perfect."

Brandon entered with the bucket of ice, and his father's coffee mug. Bob proceeded to make some strong drinks. "Hey, are we still stopping by that mailbox outlet and picking up a package from your friend in the gulf?"

Dylan lifted his drink, took a swallow, and shook his head with a 'grrr' sound. "You mean the fish? Yeah, we can't forget that. I hope Gomez packaged them well. Or at least, the people at the mailbox place don't realize they've got a load of fresh fish in their store. Might be some weird looks when we pick them up."

"That's the least of our concerns," said Bob, taking a big slug of his drink. "I'm just trying to think of anything we might have forgotten."

Dylan, taking a more measured sip this time, responded, "I think we're cool." Now looking at the penetrating rays of dawn sneaking in around the curtains of the small room he quipped, "Just another tequila sunrise."

"Not for me," said Brandon. Slamming his drink in three gulps before placing the cup on the opposite nightstand, he rolled over on the bedspread, fully dressed, before muttering, "Good night."

EIGHTEEN

U pon returning to their home in Texas, the crew checked out Dylan's website.

"Man oh man, our message board is lighting up something fierce. It looks like a call center after an 8.0 shaker. People are really responding to the post uploaded by that anonymous group, The Pacific Tribal Rioters," Dylan said, with a wink toward Bob and Brandon.

"Cool. What are they saying?" Brandon replied.

"There seems to be a consensus that we were good to not actually blow anything up. People on life support could die, thousands in the desert sweating their 'nads off with no A.C., food rotting in fridges, that kind of thing."

"We talked about that," Bob said. "Hospitals and other large outfits have their own back-up generators.

Lord knows, the casinos wouldn't experience more than a hiccup before theirs kicked in. But hey, those unnamed patriots only meant to put a scare in the powers that be, not front themselves off as actual bad guys."

The three men huddled above Dylan's laptop in the trailer he shared with Brandon back on the ranch. They continued checking the website.

"Let's see here," Dylan said, as he clicked an icon on the screen. "Looks like right now we've got forty-seven separate conversations going on The Anger Express. Some people are simply leaving their memo on the message board."

"Let me check that out," Brandon said.

"All right, here, you can sit down. Let me get up and stretch my legs a minute."

"Hey, people are on our side big time. Look at some of these posts. This guy says that pharmaceuticals are the most profitable industry in the U.S. One out of five dollars goes to the medical profession and doctors feel obligated to dispense medicine to a pill-for-any-ailment culture."

"Look at the one below," said Bob, pointing lower on the screen. "This gal says that the U.S. is only one of two countries in the whole world that allows direct prescription drug advertising to the general population. I never thought about it like that before. Those bastards get you all worked up so you'll bug your doctor for pills and injections you may not need, and that may actually harm you."

Dylan turned from the window, addressing Brandon. "Yeah, and the big drug companies have pressured Congress—the opposite of progress—to enact a law making it illegal to import pharmaceuticals from Canada. You can order anything else, just not prescription drugs. Its Big Pharma, and Big Brother, giving it to the American people where the sun don't shine. If they gave out prizes for corporate/government collusion, the pill pushers would have a trophy and awards ceremony named after them."

"That explains all of those full page, four-color ads you see in the local newspaper Uncle Joe leaves laying around the house. Not to mention all those horrible TV ads for ailments you've never heard of. What other industry can afford to do that on a regular basis? They even try to sell you a remedy for dry mouth. Why not just drink a glass of water?"

"Look what this guy wrote," said Bob, pointing to a spot farther down on the screen. "He uses the term free-range slavery, describing how you can work here or you can work there it doesn't matter; the major corporations got the whole thing sewn up. Hell, that's something I've known for years. Just never heard it expressed like that before."

"Well, you're on The Anger Express now, baby," said Dylan, a grin showing on his handsome face. "I told you, Brandon, Professor Crowder and I were right. People are angry out there. They want to get their frustrations heard, eager to yell at each other on the internet if they have to."

Brandon turned around and the two college roommates gave each other a high-five.

"That free-range slavery concept reminds me of something else I heard. It might have been Mark Twain. 'If voting worked, they wouldn't let us do it.' Say now, Dylan, are you sure they can't trace your upload at that coffee shop back to your computer and us?"

"No way. I shielded the packet with a revolving terabyte algorithm, logarithmically overwritten with a parabolic, deep-dish encryption."

Bob and Brandon looked at each other, eyebrows raised, then back at Dylan. "You sure a parabolic shallow-dish encryption wouldn't have done the trick?" Bob asked.

Dylan, at first looking a bit confused, now smiled back at his companions as Bob gave him a light brother-man punch to the shoulder.

"Can't take the chance. Its deep-dish parabolic encryption or nothing," he said, now getting the joke.

*****

"What are you boys up to?" said Julie, poking her nose in the entry of the trailer.

"Y'all be late for supper if you don't come soon," added Susan, now accompanying Julie, helping her into the double-wide mobile home.

"We're checking out the boys' website. Seems they have a lot of chatter due to some incident," answered Bob.

Susan sat down in a chair in the living room of the man cave that, from the outside, looked like an ordinary mobile home. On the inside, one could tell this habitat hadn't seen a woman's touch in some time. Julie made her way to the dining area that had been transitioned into a makeshift office, replete with a multitude of computer equipment and assorted gear. An electric guitar rested on a stand in the corner with a cord connected to an amplifier. Other wires ran from device to device throughout the room. Music streamed in across the chamber from a pair of oversized speakers tactically placed in the corners of the living room.

"Let me see," said Julie. She placed her hand on the back of Brandon's chair, leaned in and started reading posts on the screen.

"Mom, hey, you can sit here," said Brandon, rising from his seat. Julie sat down at the desk. Dylan, now with wireless mouse in hand, clicked the live-chat icon on the screen. The scene changed to a close-up image of train cars as viewed from standing outside on the boarding platform. Shown in the windows of the cars were computer-generated images of people engaged in conversations with each other. The train on the screen was sectioned off and labeled so that it was obvious who was talking to who. Suddenly, a man, appearing quite excited, shook a raised fist at his partner on the train—as detected by voice-stress analysis—and the curtains on his window closed. That section of the train faded from the screen.

"Looks like that dude told the other dude off and clicked out," said Dylan. "That's how the website works. Two people can discuss what angers them, yell at each other via live web-cam, or do whatever they want. It's better than fist fights in parking lots, or drive-by shootings."

"We've certainly seen an increase in that—back in California anyway. Doesn't seem to be so much of that around here, now that I think about it."

"You're right, Mrs. Revere. In these parts most people have guns. You don't go shooting at someone who might be armed. Lest you better have good aim, and shoot first."

"You can call me Julie, Dylan, like I've said before."

"I know, ma'am. I was just taught to show proper respect for my elders, that's all. Let's click in on these two talking here." Dylan highlighted a conversation happening in real-time on the screen.

"Yeah, those guys were cool. Those Pacific Tribal Rioters, wish I'd thought of that," said one man.

"They didn't do any actual harm, but they sure did get some attention," said the other.

Dylan looked at Brandon, who shot a concerned glance at his father. Bob was now sitting and talking with Susan in the front room. He hadn't heard the chatter on the website.

"Ain't the internet great? I've not heard about the Feds bustin' them yet. You can plant bombs, take pictures, and if you're smart the way you post it, you won't get caught," said the first speaker.

With nervous haste, Dylan clicked out of the live chat. "Hey wait. What were they talking about?" Julie wondered aloud, looking at Dylan.

"I don't know. Some prank I guess," said Dylan, again with a side-glance at Brandon.

"What did he say? What did he call them?" Julie was now giving Dylan a piercing look. "The Pacific Tribal Rioters? I remember something like that on the news. You guys were at the Gulf fishing, and Bob was doing a delivery to Vegas."

"Now that you mention it, I do remember hearing something about that on the radio," said Brandon, eyes locked with Dylan. "We were coming back from fishing with your buddy."

"Some guys put fireworks or something in the electric towers holding the power lines coming from Hoover Dam," Julie said.

"Fireworks? It's not the Fourth of July." Bob had now rejoined the group gathered at the computer.

"That's right," Dylan was quick to say. "The news reported that they found a bunch of fireworks in some electric tower down where you were, in Vegas."

"Well I'll be," said Bob, with a straight face to Dylan.

Julie, studying the exchange between the two men now broke her silence. "No, it was some kind of explosive, something that could blow out the power to Las Vegas. It caught my attention 'cause the people doing it wanted some changes done concerning medical procedures and prescription drugs. They were threatening the government. It was a warning. I also remember thinking they had a clever name. The newsman said you could take out the letters from their name, in order, and spell out the word 'patriots'."

"Yeah, I guess that is clever," said Bob, now looking at his wife. "Well, I'm glad they're blowing up stuff over at the Pacific, not around here." He was quick to change the subject and wanted to get her away from the computer. "You need some help getting up out of that chair?"

As he spoke, he placed a hand under her arm to support her. With a subdued 'aurrh,' Julie was assisted up.

"What's for dinner anyway?" he said in a raised voice, directed at Susan still sitting in the front room.

"Spaghetti 'n meatballs." She set down the computer magazine she was glancing through. "Texas style. I hope you like 'em hot."

NINETEEN

A gent Rufus Jardak Carver was sitting down in the restroom, on the third floor of the Las Vegas FBI field office when he got the text:

Conference call with the Director, meeting rm. 6, 10 min.

"Son of a bitch," he whispered to himself, "Less than six months to go. I hope I don't get caught up in some national big-case blow-jive."

Soon he found himself looking in the mirror. He washed his hands and proceeded to shape his 'fro. His wife had always told him to keep it short and forget about it. He remembered a favorite cousin in the late sixties associated with the Black Panther Party who sported a raging Afro hairdo, the kind you would hate to sit behind in a movie theater or concert hall. His was nowhere near that wild, yet, maybe after retirement, he thought to himself. He wondered for a moment what happened to his cousin, the Panther supporter. Now that it came to mind, he realized he hadn't thought of him in years. He knew there was justification in the Panther Party cause, yet he never did approve of their radical methods. Another text:

> Conference call with the Director, meeting rm. 6, 5 min.

He straightened his tie, and adjusted the .40 caber pistol strapped in a molded plastic holster under his left arm. This was balanced by the multi-pack, holding four sixteen-round magazines under his right. Not that he used his weapon much, but in this line of work, one doesn't want to be caught short. Satisfied that he appeared sufficiently presentable, Rufus proceeded to the meeting.

*****

"Hey, Chet, got your message. What's up, a conference call with the director himself?"

Chester Malcom narrowed his gaze as he answered, "That's almost right, Jay, the director herself, and I've received no head's up about it. I'm just as much in the dark as you."

R.J. Carver gave his boss a discerning look. Was this a racial taunt, or just an absentminded slip of the tongue? A few workplace verbal jabs were not unheard of in any employment environment; perhaps to be expected even more so when you worked closely with people who, at times, had your life in their hands. No, he could see there was no Uncle-Tom foolery in the man's expression. Quite the opposite, in fact.

"Oh, where's my manners? Let me introduce you to the man you'll be working with. Kevin Chan, this is Agent Carver, or Rufus Jardak Carver, or Jay, as we like to call him. "

"Pleased to meet you, Agent Carver," the young man said.

"Jay, just call me Jay. I used to threaten to beat up people that called me Rufus, except for my mom, of course. Never cared much for either first or middle names hung on me, really."

"Okay, Jay, I'm looking forward to working with you."

"That may change," Jay said. "Let's see what this is all about."

At that moment, the screen in the conference room came to life showing the official FBI seal on a waving American flag. Across the top slid the message: *INCOMING CALL.* Across the bottom, in larger bold lettering flashed: *CLASSIFIED.*

The men took their seats in the conference room. A camera faced them from the bottom of the screen. The flag and emblem faded away revealing the FBI director, Sheila Ferguson.

Ms. Ferguson was seated in her office in Washington, D.C. Outside her window, a clear blue sky was visible. She held a clicker in her hand. "Greetings, gentlemen," she said. "Hope it's not too hot out there for you today, is it?"

The three men in the Vegas office looked at each other. Chester Malcom filled the brief conversational void. "About 105 degrees all this week. Cool really. We'll manage."

Jay looked to the floor, shaking his head. The corners of his mouth turned downward.

"What's the matter, Agent Carver? You don't like the heat?" Director Ferguson asked.

"No, Ma'am, not really."

"Well, I see from your file you'll be retiring soon. Maybe then you can spend more time at the pool or in one of those air-conditioned casinos." A glint of understanding, coupled with a slight smile, ended the ice-breaking.

"All right, gentlemen, let's get down to matters at hand. There's been some disturbing activity in your area. It seems there have been postings showing pictures of explosives in electrical towers out there. Our people are duly concerned because the pictures don't appear faked. In fact, I'm told by our photographic analytical team the cardboard boxes used are quite real."

"There was something on the local news about fireworks in high-tension lines coming from the dam," Malcom said.

"That's the corrected version," the director said. "The media was ordered to change the story. One report of the actual explosive cartons did get out, but we quashed it in a hurry. We didn't want panic. There was no follow-up, so the story died, thank goodness." She clicked the remote and a picture of the explosives in the tower, as posted on the website, filled the screen.

"Actual explosives?" asked Carver, glancing at the men in the room, then back at the screen.

"Evidently so. We instructed the Clark County Sheriff's Department to hold on to one of the pieces of the boxes found by a young boy on his way home from visiting a friend. It was blowing across the road. The letters TNT were written on it, and he thought it was neat, so he kept it. His mother saw it and turned it in, thought it might be important. She was afraid it might have something to do with her son's school."

"We need more concerned citizens like her," said Malcom. Agents Carver and Chan nodded in agreement.

"Your office needs to get right on this," said the director. "Seems there was a posting on a website. Whoever did it is pushing for some changes in FDA regulations and other laws. It's kind of odd really. They don't want money, they didn't kidnap anybody and they didn't do any real damage to the transmission lines. They just want some major legislation changed, and a series of drugs and medical procedures made available."

"What, like legalizing cocaine and heroin?" Jay spoke to the image on the screen.

"No, not even an intoxicating class of drugs. Helpful medicine really, legal in other countries. Look at this." With another click of the remote, the letter Dylan had uploaded at the coffee shop and sent to the FDA and other high-ranking officials was centered on the screen.

"I'll be damned," Jay spoke under his breath.

"What was that, Agent Carver?" the voice on the screen responded.

"Uh . . . I said, what a scam . . . what a scam they've got going."

"This letter was sent to the president, members of Congress, the FDA, and some major pharmaceutical firms, among others. You check with the Clark County Sheriff and see what you can find out. It's a federal offense to threaten the power grid. Thank heaven they didn't really blow up the towers. We don't know if the redundant systems would have handled it. It could have been a major shutdown for you folks out there. Plus, it appears this website is getting a lot of activity. People are cheering this bunch on. Traffic on the site is more than eighty percent favoring the group's actions."

"Does this group have a name?" asked Malcom.

"They call themselves the Pacific Tribal Rioters. Evidently you can pull out letters, in successive order, to spell the word patriots."

The director watched as the three men in the room underwent mental gymnastics with their eyes shifting and heads bobbing, silently figuring out the letters.

"Believe me, gentlemen, the sequential letter extraction works, and they're gaining popularity. People in this town are becoming quite concerned."

Another click, and the home page image of The Anger Express website filled the screen.

"We've got our people in Houston checking up on the owners of the site where the pictures and demands first appeared. You'll be coordinating with them. Agent Carver, you'll be in charge of the investigation since the actual event occurred in your jurisdiction. Agent Chan will assist you. He's our star tech field agent, right now."

"Thank you, Director Ferguson," Kevin Chan said, as he smiled at the screen, then rubbing his hands together in his lap he looked away.

"That's about it," the director said. "Except for one thing. I don't have to tell you the lengths we go through in order to keep the people in this country safe from terrorists. This bunch, whoever did this, has a platform that is striking a chord in a large segment of the population. This situation is very upsetting to certain people in this town. I've got the president's heel on the back of my neck on this one. So as you can expect, I've got my heel, spiked as it is, on the back of yours."

"We read you loud and clear, Director Ferguson, loud and clear . . . don't we, gentlemen?"

Agents Carver and Chan nodded in agreement. "Yes, ma'am. We'll get right on it," said Carver, shooting a glance at Chan before looking back at the screen.

"You do that, Agent Carver, you get on it, and you don't worry about that retirement of yours just yet. You keep the Washington crowd happy, and you'll do fine. If not—I don't know."

Carver could tell she was looking directly at him through the satellite uplink. She raised the hand holding the clicker and with a quick finger motion, the screen went blank.

"Okay boys, you have your orders, straight from the director herself."

The three men rose from the table. "You drink coffee, Agent Chan, or is it tea?" Jay said with a grin, as he shot a glance at Chester Malcom. Malcom himself was now grinning.

"Sure, I drink coffee," said Chan.

"Then let's get a cup," said Jay. "Maybe iced coffee. If we're going to see the Sheriff, we'll hafta' go out in this God-awful heat."

TWENTY

The conference callers couldn't have had any knowledge that their supposedly secure communication had been intercepted. Unbeknownst to the agents, the level of security granted to the FBI was not the highest obtainable. Certain entities, with virtually unlimited money and power, were monitoring their every move. A subset of psychopaths, The Nightshade Group, were following this case.

"Everybody's heard of high tech," Malach Zelig said to his partner. "That's for the common herd. Above that, there's ultra-high tech. That's used in TV, radio, cell-com, GPS and modern law enforcement like Interpol and the FBI. Go a step up and you've got Omni-com, a tighter band, used by the military and many satellite applications. Then there's Odin. That's what we've got. It's tied into everything! If a cricket farts in a thunderstorm, Odin will know about it."

Jose didn't answer at first. He didn't know Malach and was suffering from jet-lag having flown in from Rio de Janeiro the night before. "That's great, amigo. Just take me to the hotel so I can rest. You can explain everything to me tomorrow." The hangover thumping in his skull, was like a bowl of rats, gnawing and pawing at the fleshy brain. Jose Ramirez was in serious need of some recuperative shut-eye.

Malach was recruited straight out of the Mossad. After serving twelve years as a highly respected field operative, he'd received a text. He'd been selected for a special unit. He could live anywhere in the world; however his territory was now North America. Also, he was told, if anything happened to him, his family in Jerusalem would be contacted. The wording made it clear that if the "something to happen" was refusing an assignment, his family would be contacted in a most unpleasant manner. This was stated even though his handlers knew refusing an assignment was not in Malach's playbook. Although the money permitted a quite lavish lifestyle, he would have gladly lived a modest existence and carried out his course of work for free.

The first assignments were the typical highly trained assassin everyday affair: sniper a congressman or poison a few industrial elites at a private meeting. Perhaps he would kidnap the child of a famous entertainer or media executive. On a good day, he might covertly stab an uncooperative Wall Street industrialist in a crowd. The usual boring fare.

This, however, was something different. Why on earth would his handlers want him to monitor the FBI as they followed the action of some crazies doing offbeat stunts posted on some silly, anti-social website? Why on earth indeed? Of one thing, Malach Zelig was certain. It had to do with the entire world.

His handlers were Globalists. Men who would stop at nothing short of total control of everything and everyone. Wealth that tall contrived political boundaries and national borders like children sketching in the sand. These were men mind-warped with power. Once the I.V. drip of absolute dominance over others started flowing, finding a nurse to extract the needle was next to impossible.

This must be it. This must be what he was told was coming. This had to be operation one-double-X-31. He'd given up trying to figure out what the operation's designation meant. That was one for the cypher nerds. But he knew that since they had called upon him, code name Azrael—in Hebrew meaning The Angel of Death—this must be a very important assignment. This was the maneuver his handlers had told him would change everything. The opportunity they'd been waiting for. This would crack the biggest nut of all, the United States of America.

TWENTY-ONE

"What did they ever do before peanut butter?" Bob said. "Talk about primitive. No wonder there were all those barbaric mongrel raids, crusades, and all that. If they just could have made themselves a proper PB&J, they could have stayed home. Everybody would've been happy and they could have avoided so much bloodshed."

"Bob, for you, bread exists only as a peanut butter delivery mechanism," Julie said with a knowing smile.

Bob took a bold stance. Lifting his right arm at an angle toward her, his hand with the index finger in the air he proclaimed: "Hey, if I were king, peanut butter would be a controlled substance. And I'll warn you right now—don't get between me and the P.B. Tis not a safe place for thee to be!"

"I'm surprised you haven't taken out an ad, wondering why the fourth decadent passion of man was left off the list of sex, drugs, and rock-n-roll."

"That's a great idea. I think I'll make up a banner and we can hang it on the side of the semi-truck trailer. We can have a number to call to have it added. You know there are only three forces in life—Love, money, and peanut butter." He licked the knife before placing it in the sink, a habit Julie detested.

"Speaking of that, Bob. I'm afraid I'm not going with you on too many more of your trucking runs. It's getting awfully hard for me to get in and out of the big rig these days."

"I've been noticing that. I've also noticed you using the cane more. Plus I see you holding on to doorjambs and countertops to keep your balance. In rock climbing, we call that three-point stabilization. Four point really, if you count the cane."

"I know. It's getting harder for me to move around, hurts more too."

"Still no word since you reapplied for the research program? You're still denied because of being in the army? At least that's what they're saying?"

"I'm afraid so. Enjoy your nighttime snack. I'm going to bed."

"Okay my dear, I'll be there in a few minutes. I'm going to check on the boys first." He kissed his wife good night. She turned and made her way to the bedroom they shared in the McKenzie house. Although he had just finished preparing one of his favorite meals, simple as it was, he couldn't help but feel dreadful about Julie's condition and wasn't tired at all.

*****

Bob made his way the twenty yards to the trailer shared by his son and Dylan McKenzie. It was still hot, long after sundown. He pulled open the screen door and knocked hard on the entry door.

"Come in!" Dylan shouted, after hearing the loud knock on the door.

"Hey guys," Bob said, his voice raised over the music. "What's up?"

"Hi Mr. R," Dylan said. Turning to Brandon, he said, "Dude, squash the tunes. We've got company."

"Oh, right." Brandon got up and made his way across the room to the stereo, beer in hand. Dylan noticed how he took a step and then another half step with the same foot.

"Dude, you're cut off, you're snowboarding," Dylan said.

"Snowboarding?" Bob, now standing nearby, asked Dylan.

"Yeah, snowboarding—you know. When you've had a couple too many and you have to take an extra step so you don't fall over. Makes it look like you're sliding as you're walking. Or snowboarding, as they say at the frat house."

Brandon lowered the volume on the stereo. Knowing his dad was watching, he walked with renewed purpose and joined the other men in the mobile-home office.

"Hi, Dad, what's up?"

"I'm not too happy with the way things are going with your mother right now. She will never admit it but she might need a wheelchair soon. She's getting worse."

"I know, she almost fell a couple of times while you were away making deliveries. I had to help her up once. She didn't want us to tell you about it. She knew you'd be upset."

"You're damn right I'm upset. Still no word on that move we made out in the desert?"

"I'm afraid not, sir. We may have to kick it up a notch. We're still getting good reviews on the website. I ran a loose analytics, and people are cheering us on roughly five to one in favor of our efforts. Most everyone agrees many things need to change in this country. Traffic on the site mentions everything from political corruption, media propaganda, endless wars enriching the mega corporations, Big Oil, and of course, our archenemy, Big Pharma. People are comparing us to Robin Hood, calling us some kind of new-age folk heroes. It's freaking great," he said smiling.

"We didn't do that little number at the towers to get your website . . . what did you call it? A bunch of unique visitors, Dylan. We did it as a last ditch effort to save Brandon's mother. She's dying, remember?"

Silence.

"You're right, sir, I know. And I've been thinking about that. We've given those scumbags more than enough time to answer our demands. I've been considering a second action. They'll most likely be watching the towers pretty heavy now, so I thought of something else."

"I can't wait," said Bob. "How about we pack up a truckload of real explosives this time and drive it into the office of the FDA? They're the ones denying her treatment. They're the ones keeping Invigratol off the market. Them and those greedy sons-of-bitches at Physbon Pharmaceuticals. I know they're wanting it released as a diet aid, billions more dollars in that."

"I know," said Dylan, "but remember, people are applauding our efforts because we're not killing anybody or wrecking anything for real."

"I don't care anymore," said Bob.

"Dad, you can't mean that," Brandon spoke up.

There was a silent pause, as the men looked back and forth at each other. Dylan was the first to speak. "Trains. I've been thinking we do something with . . . trains."

TWENTY-TWO

"Can I help you?" the attractive young deputy asked.

"I believe you can," Jay answered. "We're here to find out what you know about the incident involving explosives placed in the electrical high-voltage lines coming from the dam." Flashing his FBI identification, he looked at Agent Chan, who, now prompted, did the same.

"Just a minute, sir. Let me get the Sheriff." She picked up the phone: "Some men are here to see you, sir. They're from the FBI."

After a brief pause, a door opened and an older gentleman with a potbelly, uniformed in the garb of the Clark County Sheriff's Department, invited them into his office.

"Howdy. So you boys here from the FBI, huh? I'm Sheriff Norton. How can I help you?"

"Pleased to meet you, Sheriff. I'm Agent Carver, and this is Agent Chan. We're here investigating the incident involving the explosives in the towers."

"Sheeit, weren't much of an incident. Some punks trying to get famous making an internet video, if you ask me."

"The director takes a different view," Jay said.

"Well, weren't nothin', really. What do you mean, director?"

"The director of the FBI, Sheila Ferguson, our boss. Seems some folks in D.C. are pretty concerned as well. Concerned this . . . getting famous with internet videos, as you put it, could get out of hand," Carver said.

"They've developed quite an audience," Chan interjected.

"Weren't nuthin' but some old boxes stuffed up in the towers, as far as we can tell. I've seen the video," the sheriff explained.

"Along with a letter stating their demands?" Chan continued.

"You really think those demands will be met?"

"Don't know. That's not the point," Carver said. "People are rooting for them, calling them heroes. It's making a lot of people in Washington very nervous."

"Well you can have what we found. Just a piece of cardboard with TNT printed on it. Found by some schoolboy downwind from one of the towers. We checked the video on that website, The Anger Express. Seems the cardboard came from the same source. The lettering on the box seems to match."

"Do you still have the cardboard?"

"Of course, someone called and said you'd be here to get it."

"They did?"

"Yes, sounded official so we have it here. Been expecting you actually." Sheriff Norton reached down behind his desk and produced a plastic evidence bag containing a folded piece of cardboard. "She's all yours. Will there be anything else?"

"No, I think that will do. Thank you, Sheriff." With that, Agents Carver and Chan left the building.

"You didn't tell me they would be expecting us," said Chan, as he squinted in the afternoon sun.

"That's because nobody told me," Jay replied. He pulled out a pair of expensive wraparound sunglasses and placed them in position to shield his eyes from the harsh Nevada rays. "That's because nobody told me," he repeated, more to himself than to his partner.

*****

Malach Zelig got the text while seated on a barstool, in a fancy club in Houston.

Operation one-double-X-31: FBI on track. Monitoring progress. Further instructions to follow.

What in the name of Abraham do they want me to do? Kill a couple of FBI agents? No, that doesn't make any sense. They would just send more. He was happy Odin, the ultra-sophisticated super spy surveillance and communications network, tapped into literally everything, was doing the job of tracking his prey. What disgusting glob of scum had been puked up from the bowels of hell this time? he wondered. What evil deed were his handlers requesting? What horribly evil deed, indeed.

TWENTY-THREE

B ob asked for a few days off after his next shipment was delivered in the Rocky Mountains. He, Dylan, and Brandon, were setting out on their next David vs. Goliath act on the powers that be. The trio found themselves outside of Grand Junction, Colorado. They had fibbed to Julie and Susan, telling them they were going camping for a few days after Bob made a delivery in Denver. As usual, if there was no pressing need, Bob's boss didn't care if he brought the semi back right away, as long as the delivery was on time. Once again they rented a car with Dylan's fake I.D. This time it was a green SUV, 4x4, as specified by their master-of-tricks, Dylan McKenzie. They stopped at sporting outlet before heading out of town and in due course were rough riding off the highway, down an obscure dirt road.

"This'll do," Dylan said. "I did my homework. The tracks should be just beyond that ridge."

Brandon pulled the 4x4 into some bushes. "This is crazy," he said, turning to Dylan.

"Crazy is as crazy does," Dylan replied. He turned and spoke over his shoulder, his voice raised, "Wake up, Bob. Gang's all here."

Bob shook himself into consciousness. "What the hell? Where are we?" He looked around at the veil of green encompassing the vehicle. "Are you sure we need all this stuff?" Bob asked, now considering the equipment cramping his quarters.

"Pretty sure," Dylan replied. "Let's load up."

The men exited the SUV and gathered the materials purchased at the sporting goods store. They split up the items into backpacks for the hike through the woods. Included were a climbing harness, ropes, a crossbow, two life vests, some fishing line, a kayaking helmet, a motorcycle helmet, and a head mount video camera. Also contained within were a crowbar, three bottles of water, and a Taser.

The sun was at its highest point in the sky when the three men set off into the woods. Following an adrenaline-infused hike, they came to a spot overlooking some railroad tracks and the Colorado River.

"This'll do," Dylan said, after checking his watch. "See that tree, it's perfect." The crew stood on a ledge some thirty feet above the rails. "Give me the crossbow." Bob and Brandon watched as Dylan skillfully loaded the bow and attached the line used for bow-fishing. Aiming high over the railroad tracks, just past a split in the branches, he let one fly. It sailed through the tree and stopped short when Dylan clamped down on the line trailing from the bow. The arrow shaft swung like a pendulum in mid-air, almost touching the ground above the tracks. "Brandon, bro, go grab that bolt and bring it back here, will ya?"

"Bolt?"

"Yeah, bolt. That's what they call a crossbow arrow. Go get it will you? Hurry now, we don't have much time."

Brandon scrambled down the dirt embankment, and onto the tracks to retrieve the bolt.

"Be careful. Don't break the fishing line," Dylan called after him.

Dylan could see that his buddy was having trouble getting back up the sloped railroad embankment. "Here, Bob, hold this." He handed Bob the crossbow and made his way to the edge of the woods where the railroad line was cut into the mountain. He retrieved the bolt from his roommate and hastily tied the end of a ¼-inch rope to the fishing line, after biting the line with his teeth. Working his way back up the side of the hill, he reached Bob.

"Put on your harness and backpack. The train will be here any minute."

With great care not to break the fishing line, Dylan pulled the ¼-inch rope, guiding it through the bough of the tree.

"Why didn't you just attach the climbing rope to the fishing line?" Brandon asked, having rejoined his companions.

"Too heavy. Couldn't risk the climbing rope getting caught and breaking the fishing line." A flock of birds took off from a point two miles up the tracks from their location. "Bob, you ready? We've only got one shot at this; it should work just fine, I saw it in a movie."

Dylan tied the climbing rope to the ¼-inch line, and pulled it through the tree and over the strong branch overhanging the tracks. Bob looked at Dylan, then back at Brandon. "Shouldn't it be one of you doing this?" he said. "If I don't make it . . . tell your mom I love her. I wish I could do something else but . . ."

"No time," Dylan interrupted. "Get over here. Let me get you clipped on. Brandon, you ready? Throw the rope around that stump behind you as an anchor and GET READY!"

Bob stood by the ledge wearing his backpack. Before donning the backpack, with a kayak helmet clipped to it, he had strapped himself into the mountain-climber's harness. He also wore sports padding on his knees, elbows, shins, and shoulders. The ensemble was finished off, and nicely accessorized, with thick leather gloves and a full-faced motorcycle helmet. Soon the train made its way past the men overlooking it, and set for action. "Remember," Dylan said. "We need the people behind us. This plan should work if there are no slip-ups."

"Yeah," Bob said, gripping the rope with both hands, "no slip-ups." He studied the train below. He could see up the tracks; most of the cars coming his way were shipping-container rail cars.

"You better go!" Dylan shouted to be heard above the roar of the train. "The longer you wait, the farther you'll have to go to get to the engineer."

"You're right!" Bob shouted back. "You ready?" he asked, with one last look at Dylan, and another slightly longer look at Brandon. His only son was now braced with his feet plowed into the dirt, holding his end of the rope around the tree stump. With a, "Here goes nothing," Bob swung out into space over the passing train. With Bob still swinging in midair, Dylan and Brandon lowered him to just above the undulating mass of steel. At just the right moment, Bob pulled the special ripcord Dylan had rigged, and dropped onto a rusted shipping container. He rolled a bit before spread-eagling himself, stopping his motion.

*****

Kyle Charles Jones never really forgave his father for giving him first and second names that started with K and C. Being the fourth in his family to be in the railroad business though, it did seem somewhat appropriate. His dad had gotten him his dream job. He liked his work as a freight train engineer. He was enjoying it even more on this beautiful day, riding along while having a smoke with the window open on the locomotive. He knew he most likely wouldn't be caught breaking regulations, but he kept the window on the door open, just for good measure. Approaching a bridge on a curved section of tracks, he had slowed the train down to the required fifteen miles an hour. Surprise would be an understatement, when a man wearing a backpack, an assortment of mismatched plastic protective gear, and a motorcycle helmet with a darkened visor and attached camera stuck a Taser through the window.

It was hard to hear over the sound of the engine and the muffling effect of the full-face helmet, but he understood the words.

"Don't move. If I pull the trigger, you'll be zapped with fifty-thousand volts, and you'll squeal like a stuck pig. I don't want to hurt you and we're not going to crash the train. Just do what I say and you'll be okay."

Kyle started to reach into his back pocket. The man responded by sticking the weapon farther into the engine cab and raised the visor on his helmet a crack before yelling, "DON'T DO IT! And don't touch the controls!"

Kyle ceased his hand motion and backed away from the weapon as the well-armored man reached in the window and released the latch opening the door. As he made his way into the compartment, the crowbar sticking out of his backpack clanged on the metal doorframe. Ducking a bit, he wiggled his way inside. After clearing all the other equipment clipped to his backpack, he stood, still pointing the Taser at Kyle.

"What the hell is this?" Kyle said. "Am I getting punked? Did Jessy put you up to this? Is that thing for real?"

"Sure is. If I have to light you up, I'll be your daddy and you'll be dancing to a whole new tune, and singing the blues, in the house of pain. Don't make me do it. Just think of this as a big publicity stunt," Bob said, as he switched on the camera.

"Where'd you come from? How'd you get here anyway?"

"Tarzan style. I'm wearing this get-up in case I missed and bounced my ass off the train into the dirt."

"Well, what the freak is going on, man? You really can't hijack a train you know! It's got to run on railroad tracks."

"We're shooting a video and you're the star. Now give me your phone."

Kyle reached into his back pocket, producing his smartphone, and handed it to Bob.

"Thank you. Won't be needing this right now," Bob said, as he tossed the phone out the window.

"Hey, what the . . . "

"Don't worry about it. It wouldn't be any good after it got wet anyway."

"Got wet?"

"Yeah, got wet, when we jump in the river."

"Jump in the river?"

"That's right! Here put on this life jacket and this kayaking helmet. You'll be fine."

"I still don't get it."

"Look up ahead, see those boxes in the middle of the bridge? That's high explosives, except not really. We're proving we could drop a mile long trainload of useless consumer crap into the river and not hurt a soul doing it—as long as we rescued you in the process."

Kyle looked out his side of the train, and saw the boxes piled up in the middle of the span. Bob zoomed in on the cases of explosives, then zoomed out, refocusing the camera on Kyle.

"Have I hurt you? Talk into the camera. People are going to see this. You'll be a celebrity."

"No, I'm okay."

"Do you agree that if we blew the bridge after you and I jumped into the river, you would live to talk about it? All while watching millions of dollars of other people's money being wasted into a watery oblivion."

"Yeah, I guess."

"Good," Bob said as he got out of his backpack and unstrapped the protective sporting gear he was wearing. "All right, we're almost to the bridge. Put this baby in neutral, or shut off the engine, whatever you have to do to just leave this sucker parked on the tracks. Then we jump."

"Jump?

"That's right. We jump and leave the train right here. It'll coast to a stop and they can come retrieve it. No real harm done. We're just making a point."

Bob could see that the young engineer was fully compliant with all his commands. Donning the life jacket and helmet, he had offered no resistance. Bob could also tell by now the trainman seemed quite intrigued with the whole affair. He dropped the backpack on the metal floor of the cab and the protruding crowbar made another loud clang. After attending to his own life jacket, he opened the door and guided his obedient captive out onto the running board of the locomotive. He picked up the backpack and exited the cab of the engine.

"Hey, what was the crowbar all about?"

"Didn't know you'd have the window down. Thought I might have to pry open a door or something."

"Yeah, I was having a smoke so I opened up the wind . . . wait a minute, who'd you say is going to see this video?"

"Everybody, my friend, everybody. You can bet on it. Now JUMP!" With that, Bob gave Kyle a gentle push off the train. The two men dropped fifteen feet into the slow-moving water. Jumping at the same time, he looked at the engineer, who was now looking back into the camera.

"Everybody—holy crap! My boss is gunna . . ."

With a double splash, they hit the water. Seeing Kyle make his way to the closest shore, Bob let himself drift downstream a ways before removing the motorcycle helmet that concealed his face. Before he was out of shouting range he yelled, "Check out social media and videos posted on the internet! You'll be famous!"

Kyle, now standing on the riverbank, watched the strangely-dressed, yet very likeable man who'd interrupted his regular work day, drift away in the current. He waved an animated goodbye while shouting back. "Yeah okay, I'll look for it, man, cool!" Now turning and making his way through the bushes, he knew his superiors would be monitoring the train with GPS. Upon seeing it stopped on a bridge in the middle of nowhere, help would soon be on the way.

TWENTY-FOUR

D ylan and Brandon hiked back through the woods after gathering up all evidence of the trapeze act above the railroad tracks. They swept a branch across the trail in random dirt spots on the path to obscure footprints. This was unnecessary on the many imbedded stone slabs along their route, which made that part of the hike much quicker. After their return to the SUV, the two roommates made haste to the pick-up location downriver.

Brandon pulled up close to the water's edge. Bob was standing with his shirt drying on a rock above the dripping backpack and motorcycle helmet. "How'd it go, Dad? Everything all right? You get some good footage?"

"Yeah, it went good. I might have sprained my wrist landing on the boxcar or shipping container, whatever it was, but I'll be fine. I got some good video. In fact, I think the engineer kind of liked the whole experience. He seemed almost happy to be involved, even filmed. Except he may have some explaining to do about an open window."

"That sounds great, Dad. You ready to go?"

"Yeah, Mr. R. Let's go, it's pumpkin time! No telling when the authorities might roll up. We better get the hell out of here. And out of this whole state in fact, pretty as it is."

Bob grabbed the items off the rock and piled in. Brandon put it in gear and headed out of the wooded river access. "Anybody see you come out of the water, ask you what happened to your boat, or anything?" inquired Dylan.

"No, not a soul around. We picked a good spot. I ditched the crowbar. Didn't need it, thankfully. It's found a new home at the bottom of the river."

After turning in the SUV, heading back in the big rig involved the men reliving the little escapade they'd pulled off and verbally patting each other on the back.

"I'll tell you, Dylan," Bob said after a while. "It's only in my wildest dreams that this whole scheme of yours, antagonizing the government and all, will work."

"You know what they say," Dylan answered. "If you don't wake up and pursue your dreams, you might as well stay asleep."

"Yeah, I guess you're right," Bob said, and then, looking out the side window repeated, "I guess you're right."

*****

During dinner with Susan, Julie, and Demo Joe McKenzie, the travelers recounted the trip in the big rig and a made-up story of camping outside of Denver. Brandon helped Susan with the dishes, as Dylan and Bob retired to the mobile home shared by the college buddies.

Dylan had already edited the video in the big rig on the journey home. He'd altered Bob's voice using software found on the internet.

The trio uploaded the video of the exploit on the train, along with another copy of the letter stating their demands involving Invigratol, Physbon Pharmaceuticals, and the FDA, at a Wi-Fi hot spot along the way. Once again, Dylan, being the computer whiz kid, utilized sophisticated encryption methods making the upload untraceable. The laptop, after being electronically wiped, was now in a thousand pieces, having been tossed out the window as the men rounded a five-hundred foot cliff.

"People are already cheering our efforts on the train," Dylan said after logging onto the website. "Check out what they're saying now. Here's a story about an old man feeding the homeless in Florida.

He's been charged with a crime, could get sixty days in jail and a $500 fine for helping people. Here's another one about how the justice system preys upon the poor, jacking a $25 failure to notify the DMV of address change to a $2,300 fine of combined fees and penalties."

"Hey, scroll on down. What's this?" Bob asked.

"Wow, you recall that 61-year-old mailman who delivered 535 letters to Washington by landing his gyrocopter on Capitol Hill? I remember because that's the room number of our computer lab. He was a concerned citizen wanting to end government corruption. He said he didn't want to hurt anybody—just make a statement. People are comparing us to him, but saying we're doing it a whole lot better."

"I remember that guy. I don't think the hamster was spinning the little wheel in his dome quite up to speed, if you know what I mean."

"I know what you mean. Some say his lampshade might have concealed a rather dim bulb," Dylan said. "But he had balls. Said a kid with a BB gun could have shot him down. Most of his flight was only thirty to forty feet off the ground. He never even registered a blip on NORAD's radar while flying for miles. Here's another one about a gal completing courses as an R.N. who can't get a job because she doesn't speak Spanish. She wonders why we have to speak the language of foreigners to be employed in our own country. Hell, it's been that way here in Texas for years."

"You don't have to tell me," Bob said. "How much time did you give those bastards to respond to our plea?"

"Ten days," Dylan replied. "If they don't have some kind of response to us via the lame-stream media in ten days, we'll give them a lot more to worry about than a bunch of useless retail crap dumped in a river. That's for sure."

"I don't think I want to know your next plan, Dylan. You got any whiskey around here?"

"You know where it is."

"I think I'll pour myself a tall one. You can find me on the porch, having a smoke if you want . . . damn, last one. I just opened this pack yesterday."

TWENTY-FIVE

Bob was on another out-of-state run. Brandon and Dylan were at a neighbor's property helping cut down some trees to clear an area for a new barn. Julie, being tired of bouncing off the walls, literally and figuratively, was out shopping with a friend she had met in a local writers' group. Old Demo Joe was in town playing Texas Hold-Em, and drinking at a saloon owned by a close friend.

Information not readily shared amongst the McKenzie family, or others, was that Joe McKenzie had not been officially married to his wife, Ann. It seemed that during a rather inebriated trip to Las Vegas in his younger days, he had joined a former girlfriend in holy matrimony at an all-night, drive-through wedding chapel. Neither could remember, nor explain, the cheesy finger rings, cheap flowers, or balloons they found in their hotel room the next morning amongst the overturned beer and tequila bottles. They assumed they'd been involved in some sort of bazaar casino ritual and laughed it off.

When Joe and Ann eloped years later and discovered that their wedding could not proceed, they instituted a mock ceremony and agreed they would make it legal one day soon. That day never arrived. Consequently, when Joe moved into Ann's sizeable ranch house, the one he now occupied, everyone thought things were as they should be.

Joe had kept his business address at the warehouse a few miles away, driving there most mornings, or leaving town to 'bring down another one' as he liked to say. When Ann passed away, leaving no siblings, the ranch became the legal property of Dylan and Susan. Ann's death corresponded closely with Joe's failing health, and as a result, him having to shut down his business. With no reason to keep volatile supplies in a location so far away, he hired some friends to move his considerable stash of explosives to a steel storage building, specially built, on the ranch. These events, while isolated from each other, had the collective result of there being no public record of Joe ever having lived on the property, and no official document of the items stored there.

*****

Agent Carver knocked on the door to the McKenzie Home.

"Hello, can I help you?" Susan asked, opening the door.

"Good afternoon. My name is Agent Carver," Jay said, while holding out his I.D. "and this is Agent Chan." The younger tech-savvy agent did the same. "May we come in?"

Susan was silent for a moment. "FBI, y'all are from the FBI! Goodness gracious, whatever could be the trouble? Why certainly, come in. I never thought I'd be talking to the FBI. What can I help you gentlemen with?"

"We're investigating an incident that occurred in the Nevada desert. Some individuals placed dynamite boxes in the high-voltage lines outside of Las Vegas. They then took pictures and uploaded them to a website. A website with an I.P. address registered to this location. Do you know anything about that?"

"My brother, Dylan, has a website he started. But I don't know much about it. It has to do with people yelling at each other. Getting stuff off their chest, as he would say."

"Is your brother here now?" Chan inquired.

"No, 'fraid not. He's out cutting down trees at a friend's house."

"You mind if we look around a bit?" Carver asked, peering out the window.

"No, but I don't see why."

"What's that mobile home right out there?" Carver asked.

"That's Dylan's place. I can't let you go in there. My brother would kill me. Don't y'all need a warrant or something, to go poking around?"

"What about that steel-sided building way down there?" Carver asked, ignoring her question.

"Oh that. That's just where my uncle keeps some old supplies and stuff. Ain't nothing special, really."

"Any idea when your brother will be back? We'd like to ask him a few questions."

"After sundown, I suspect. Unless they stay at Ernie's place to have a few beers."

"Okay, Miss, thank you for your time," said Carver. "Let's go, Kevin, we've done all we can here." Stepping outside, the two federal agents descended the steps, got in their car and drove away.

*****

"She knows something," Carver said as he turned off the long gravel road and onto the highway. "I can smell it. Did you see the way she flinched when we mentioned dynamite boxes? I'll tell you, Chan, I've gone up against the mob, white supremacists, bank robbers, human traffickers, and drug dealers. I've investigated international art theft rings, counterfeiters, money laundering, and interstate mass-murderers. I'm telling you, she knows something."

*****

Malach Zelig received a text while in the lounge at the shooting range. He'd just grouped four full clips from a .45 caliber Colt 1911 in three-inch circles, at twenty-five yards.

> Operation one-double-X-31 update: Target is go. Secure provisions. Proceed to destination. Execution zero hr. morning of 11-9.
>
> Failure N-A-O.

He knew that failure was not-an-option. That's why they called on him. He checked his calendar, figured how long it would take to drive to San Francisco at a safe highway speed and picked up his gym bag. Before a surprise visit at the McKenzie ranch, he would need a few additional items.

TWENTY-SIX

Code name Azrael made a few calls. He picked up two ram-air parachutes, some dependable wireless detonators, an Uzi, and a few boxes of ammo. His orders were clear, up to a point. Appropriate the necessary supplies and proceed to the San Francisco Bay area. Further instructions to follow.

Jose Ramirez had been recruited by the Nightshade Group for his exceptional work as a freelance house painter employed by the South American drug cartels. The traditional color left on the walls where he plied his trade was red—blood red. The dark hair and eyes positioned north of an appealing smile concealed an opaque soul, a black hole where human spirits circled the event horizon only to be sucked inside and never seen again. He was the Latino counterpart to Malach, partnered with him for this special two-man operation. The duo worked together almost telepathically.

*****

Maggie was awakened by soft footsteps on the gravel outside. Exiting the residence through her doggie door, she saw a man dressed in black. Closer still, she encountered a two-pound chunk of medium cooked rib-eye steak. Twenty minutes later, having chomped down the delicious hunk, she was back inside. With the barbiturates now kicking in, she was sprawled out on the floor, quickly easing her way into doggie dreamland.

Dylan and Brandon had mysteriously received anonymous tickets to a favored rock band playing in Austin, about two hours away. It was also the night when Julie had her bi-monthly meeting with her writers group.

Susan was known to spend most evenings in her room alone when Brandon was away. She usually wore headphones for her tablet or laptop as her elder uncle, being hard of hearing, had the TV up loud.

*****

As Jose picked the lock to the storage building, Malach stood silent, Uzi in hand. They had brought special portable conveyor ramps with rubber coated metal wheels to facilitate the loading of boxes into the RV—the vehicle Bob had parked behind the storage shed upon his and Julie's arrival. The box loading was made easier by the removal of three siding panels on the modified steel structure with a cordless screwdriver. The pinch had been planned for this evening because Bob would be trucking his way through Albuquerque, New Mexico, right about now. With the nearest neighbor a fifteen-minute walk away, the two men worked undisturbed, moving boxes of TNT, C4, and plastique explosive out of the shed and into the RV.

*****

One of the curses of old age is a person tends to require less sleep. It had finally cooled off some after a long triple-digit summer in southern Texas. Joe McKenzie awoke and decided he would get some fresh air. It was just after midnight when he worked his feet into a pair of slippers. Standing on the porch, he could see the pale reflection of a dark sedan parked on the frontage road to his property. Realizing something was amiss, he retrieved the 12 gauge held in reserve in a closet by the front door. Feeling well able to defend himself against any malevolent teenagers crossing the property to take a dip in his pond, he decided now might be a good time for a security check—out by way of the parked car.

The autumn leaves, an enchanting retina blast of color in the daylight, registered only as sharp crunches underfoot as he got closer to the unoccupied late model black sedan. Closer still revealed the four freshly cut strands of barbed wire in the fence defining his property. He looked around before proceeding to the rear of the estate.

As he got closer to the large metal shed, he could see light flickering through the roof vents. Slowing his pace while raising the shotgun, Joe rounded the back corner of the storage building.

"Hey, what the . . . "

A quick three-round burst of lead was discharged as a triple series of soft puffs, hitting its mark.

Demo Joe dropped the scattergun and hit the ground clutching his chest. His eyes widened on his assailant as a final squirt of crimson spurt through his fingers. He tried to speak but couldn't make a sound.

Joe McKenzie would never again suffer the anguish of a shortened sleep cycle.

TWENTY-SEVEN

S usan arose to find Maggie's bowl hadn't been placed in the usual location. This indicated she hadn't been fed yet by Uncle Joe. Also, Maggie seemed strangely undisturbed by the motion of opening blinds, brewing coffee and general kitchen activities, a morning routine Susan dutifully assumed in the household.

A look out the window revealed a set of large tire tracks from the rear sector of the property leading to a break in the barbwire fence along the frontage road. Dylan's truck was parked by his trailer, but Julie's small white sedan was nowhere in sight. Susan realized Julie should be awake by now, and after a light knock on her bedroom door, she peeked inside. The bed was made but there was no Julie. She went to check on Uncle Joe. Upon not finding him anywhere inside, she proceeded to call on her brother. Something was definitely awry on the McKenzie estate.

After a couple rounds of loud knocking on the front door of Dylan's mobile home, Susan let herself in. She found her brother folded over the computer keyboard, while Brandon was bagging heavy Zs on the couch. Evidently, a few Texas Long-Necks had been instrumental in enabling the pair into a deep sleep.

"Dylan, wake up. I think something's wrong. I can't find Uncle Joe," she said shaking him into fuzzy-brained awareness.

"What?"

"I said I can't find Uncle Joe. Or Brandon's mom, either."

"Maybe they're out by the pond, or around back, or somewhere with the dog."

"I don't think so. Brandon's mother's car isn't here and there's strange tracks from the shed to the road. Also, it looks like the fence has been cut."

"Strange tracks, the fence cut, what are you talking about?" Dylan pulled a cushion from a chair beside him and threw it on his slumbering roommate. "Wake up, dude, you need to get your butt up off the couch."

Susan explained the morning's circumstances as the two men donned footwear and pushed stringy hair out of yawning faces. They picked up their cellphones before going outside.

While walking toward the tracks in the expansive front yard of the property, Brandon called his mother. "Mom, what's up? Where are you?"

"I'm at Bonnie's house. Our writers' meeting went overtime. When I went outside I had a flat tire. I called her and she came and got me. You were at the concert and it was too late and long of a drive for her to take me home, so she put me up here. We figured you could come out in the morning and change tires for me."

"Yeah, okay, that's no problem. At least I don't think so—hang on Mom, let me call you back. I'm glad you're alright, I'll call you back, don't worry, we'll get your car fixed—love you."

With the call abruptly ended, Brandon put the phone in his pocket and turned to see what had caught Dylan's attention. From the vantage point of about five hundred feet now, roughly halfway from the main house, they had gained a view around some low bushes at the back of the storage shed. Brandon could see a figure lying on the ground clad in a familiar flannel robe and slippers. As Susan shrieked, she and Dylan ran toward the figure.

Dylan rolled Uncle Joe onto his back and the hand covering the blood-soaked chest wound flopped beside the body. He reached down and closed the eyelids preventing the dead man from staring in grotesque fashion at his sobbing niece. Dylan stood up, put his arms around Susan and looked at Brandon.

Brandon, brow furrowed, stood in silence, returning his stare. After a long pause, the two young men considered the two metal panels lying in the sand beside the tire tracks, leading away from the wide-open shed. Only a few dust covered odds and ends and about twenty empty TNT boxes remained inside. The explosives had all been removed.

Susan, having pulled away from her brother, surveyed the damage.

"Looks like a robbery gone bad, real bad," Dylan said.

"I guess this explains those anonymous concert tickets," Brandon responded with a pained expression on his face. "Someone wanted us out of here so they could steal the explosives, but who? Who knew that stuff was here? You told me nobody knew about it except for family, and a few very close friends."

"That's right," Dylan answered. "Nobody knew we had that stuff except lifelong friends of Joe's and the ones that live here now. Plus, why steal your folks RV? Seems a flatbed would've been better. Easier and quicker to load. Also, now that I think about it, your father wasn't here either. Whoever sent us those tickets knew that Bob would be out of town."

Susan, now having composed herself, spoke up.

"I was tired the other day and went to bed early. Y'all weren't here anyway so I forgot to tell you. The FBI was here. They were asking about your website and something to do with boxes of dynamite stuck in electrical towers." She looked up into the troubled face of her older brother and asked, "You don't think this has anything to do with that, do you?"

TWENTY-EIGHT

D ylan picked up the shotgun. He took a look about the property. Reassuring himself the worst had passed, he ejected the live rounds into the sand, picked them up, and addressed his sister.

"The FBI was here? Why didn't you tell me?"

"I just told you why I didn't tell you."

"Yeah, alright, I heard you. Okay, what'd they say?"

"They asked about your website and said something about dynamite boxes in towers in the desert."

"What'd you say?"

"Nothing, really. I told them I didn't know anything, because I don't. What's going on, Dylan? Uncle Joe is dead. What are we gunna do?" Dylan could see the emotions well up inside her again.

"Why didn't you call me?"

"I figured you wouldn't hear the phone over the chainsaw, and I'd tell you when you got home. You guys were late and I went to bed. The next morning it skipped my mind, I guess."

"The FBI shows up asking about explosives and my website and you forgot about it?"

"I'm sorry," she said, starting to cry again. "But wait, you can't be mad at me. Uncle Joe is dead. What the fuck's going on?" Tears were now streaming down her face. "What have you been up to?"

"Nothing."

"Nothing? Seems awfully funny, Dylan. They said that there were pictures of dynamite boxes in electrical towers by Las Vegas. They said they knew the pictures were on your website."

"I can't help it if people put stuff on the website. That's what it's for. That, and live two-way chat. What did you tell them? What else did they want?"

"They wanted to look around. I told them they needed a warrant."

"Well, that's good."

Brandon broke in, attempting to ease the tension. "We better call the cops, dude. Your uncle's dead and there's been a burglary."

With a clenched jaw and narrowed eyes, Dylan considered the statement. "Yeah, but nobody knows about all the stuff Joe had rat-holed in here. Our uncle used to give some of it to good friends at times, to blow out tree stumps and boulders on their properties. That's it!"

"Hey, not to sound like a wise guy, but he can't get into any trouble now. What if we put the panels back on and it'll just look like somebody stole the RV? The cops won't have any reason to ask about explosives."

"It's not the cops I'm worried about. It's the FBI."

Susan, silently studying the two roommates, now spoke. "I thought you said you had nothing to worry about with the FBI, Dylan? You said you were doing nothing wrong?"

"Look Sue, it doesn't matter. If they think something is up, they can find something to bust us on. Those pictures were on the website, we saw them. We talked about them. We, I mean, Uncle Joe, did have a bunch of dynamite and stuff here and now it's gone along with Bob and Julie's motorhome, and Joe is dead. I think Brandon is right, we should put the shed back together and just deal with this thing as a homicide and vehicle theft. That's plenty for the cops to handle and it makes sense. Let's leave the whole warehouse full of explosives, now gone, out of it. We could all be in trouble. Illegal storage of unregistered high explosives, possession of bomb-making materials, who knows? Everything changed after the twin towers came down. Remember this ranch is on the books with our names on the deed. They could say you already lied to them because actually—you did.

You knew what Joe had in there. You don't want to go to jail, do you?"

Susan's eyes widened while taking in her brother's serious air. After a quick look at Brandon, his expression just as serious, she answered.

"No."

"Alright then. We've got no time for mourning this morning. Brandon, bro, do me a favor, pick up all of these sheet metal screws you can find laying around here. We've got some left over from the builders, but it's better if we use the old weathered ones first. Comb the sand to find as many as you can. Sue, maybe you help him."

They were startled like an alarm going off in an ICBM silo when Brandon's cell phone rang. The trio looked at each other as he accepted the call.

"Yeah. Hi, Mom, no I haven't forgot about you. Something came up, something bad." He studied Dylan who, returning the glance, gave a slight nod of his head. "It's better I don't tell you on the phone but alright. Joe's dead—somebody shot him and stole you and dad's motorhome. I don't know. Look, I'm with Dylan and Susan right now. We've got to call the police and try and figure this thing out. I'll probably be out there in a couple of hours. You and Bonnie have breakfast or something—I know—I love you, too."

"Here, let me have one of those screws, I'll match it up with the right bit and get my battery-powered drill. I guess it doesn't matter about the shotgun. It looks like it wasn't fired, but I better keep it handy to show the cops. I'll take it inside."

"Brandon," Susan said, somewhat more composed, "I can't pick up screws with my dead uncle lying ten feet away. You can do it. I'm going in to feed the dog."

The metal siding panels had been laid one on top of the other in the order of their removal. It wasn't difficult to reinstall the pieces back into their original position, with the recovered screws. The few new screws were hidden in the uncut grass growing up against the building. Efforts had been taken to make the area appear normal. As normal as possible with the dead body of an old man in pajamas and slippers laying at the corner of the structure.

Bob was expected back the following day for a layover before his next delivery. Dylan and Brandon had decided not to call him lest he say something about their secret exploits on the phone. The concern, at this time, was their phones might be tapped. They agreed while driving to do the tire change on Julie's car to let her make the call and inform him of the shooting on the ranch. They knew he wouldn't say anything to her.

Leading up to Bob's return were conversations with homicide detectives, the coroner, funeral directors, necessary friends, and a contractor to repair the fence. With internment decided, the three collaborators had a serious sit-down in Dylan's double-wide upon Bob's return.

"Jesus Christ, Dylan, this thing's gotten way out of hand. I knew it was a shot in the dark—oh my God, I'm so sorry, I didn't mean . . . I meant to say . . . I knew the odds were against us to help Brandon's mother, but I never dreamed anything like this would happen." The tension in Bob's voice was palpable.

"I know."

"You said you had another plan if the train thing got no response. I say forget it, this whole deal has gone way too far. I must've been insane to let you talk me into this hair-brained scheme. Jeeze man, I don't know what to say. Forgive me, Dylan—I know it wasn't your fault. I'm so sorry about what happened to Joe, really."

"Yeah, I know, so am I. On the other hand, I'll tell you something. Joe always said he counted his lucky stars every time a building came down and nobody got hurt. Said he figured one day a spark, static electricity, or some dumb mistake would have his fleshy parts blown hither and yon. He always thought he'd be strewn about the county like confetti out of a party popper. Yet it never happened. But it looks like he might've been right, in a way; those things that go boom got him in the end. Just not the way he expected."

"Maybe we should move out of here," Bob continued. "Your family has done enough, more than enough for us already."

"No way," Dylan protested. "Especially now. We can't let our uncle's passing scare us away. We're all in, as he would say. Plus he'd been telling me he kind of knew his time was near. Said getting old wasn't for the faint of heart. Said he was ready for the alternative. Besides, y'all are on course to be . . . family, real family." He shot a glance at Brandon, who, blushing a tad, couldn't stifle a slight nod.

"Plus the fact Joe would've wanted us to go on. He didn't show it much but he was the southern rebel type. I learned most of my contempt for the Feds from him. I'm willing to bet if he knew what we were doing and why, he'd be the first one to donate real explosives to the cause."

"Dylan, wake up man, they're on to us. You might have plenty of dislike for the government, and I agree, but the fricken FBI showed up on your property! They knew about the towers," Brandon said.

"True, but they didn't connect any old TNT boxes to us. That shows they're grasping at straws. The website posts are untraceable. I made sure of that. As for the police, I don't think they'll be looking very hard. A few years ago, Joe wrote some letters to the editor of the local paper pointing out the shortcomings of a few homegrown politicians and the chief of police. They'll probably just make some calls, then chalk it up to meth freaks wanting to snag a free RV to haul somewhere out in the boonies."

"Yeah," Brandon interjected, "now that you mention it, they didn't seem too curious, or ask too many questions. I got the feeling they didn't really care. I just thought it was because he was old and they were too busy."

"We need to honor Joe's memory and we're still trying to save your mother's life. Give me your phones." Without argument, or inquiry, the father and son handed Dylan their cell phones.

"You realize, don't you, all communication leaves crumbs that can be charted back to the user. I digi-stitched an analogue fade and evap disrupter tail to a crypto-mutated virus I cloned. It leapfrogs every two-tenths of a second."

Bob and Brandon exchanged glances, eyebrows raised. They watched as Dylan inserted a cord from his computer into their phones, one after another. Upon completion of a few keystrokes and mouse clicks, the phones were returned.

"There you go. I call it strip-script. It encodes, and then erases, any call, text message, voice mail or anything. You guys think I'm just playing with my 'puter late at night. In reality, I'm working, building software for the masses. This is a prototype, but I've already checked it out. It's like a knight wearing titanium armor over Kevlar skivvies. Makes your phones impervious to outside attack.

"We've got to be extra careful now," Dylan continued. "The FBI are pretty predictable but whoever sent those tickets and ripped Joe's stash did it with three well-placed gunshots nobody heard. They're still out there, and I have yet to reason why they stole your old RV. Hell, a moving van would've been quicker, and easier to load. Must've had some reason . . . must've had a damn good reason."

THIRTY

Carver and Chan had been occupying the special agent guest office at the Houston FBI Headquarters. This was an established workroom for two or more out-of-town agents available in all of the big city FBI buildings. Agents were allowed to set up, access files, interview persons of interest and conduct necessary business relating to their current case.

Chan entered the office flipping through a manila folder. "Got the lab tests back. You were right. The boxes at the towers and the ones on the railroad bridge above the Colorado River were from the same shipment. It says here that trace amounts of identical phosphorous nitrate, extracted from the cardboard, were found in each sample."

"Let me see that," Carver said, taking the folder from his partner. "See these figures? That is a reference number to the chemical tracer put in the explosives. Access the database. I want to know who made this stuff and, more importantly, who it was sent to."

"Right away, chief," Chan said with a slight smile and a nod as he turned and walked away.

"I'm not the chief. I'm not even the deputy chief," Carver called after him. "I'm just a guy trying to solve one last case, and hopefully, secure my pension."

*****

Carver's cell phone rang. "Hey, son."

"Hi, Dad. I've been following the exploits on that group, The Pacific Tribal Rioters. Everyone in the dorm has. It's big news. You don't know anything about that, do you?"

"As a matter of fact I do. It's my case, Jonah. But you know I can't really discuss it."

"Wow, cool. A lot of the gang here hangs out on The Anger Express website. We see what's going on. We know this country is all fu . . . I mean—all screwed up."

"Yeah, what else is new?" Carver said, using a common phrase but in reality hoping to change the subject.

"I saw on a news feed that the governor of California slammed a pharmaceutical company for raising its price on a lifesaving drug more than five-hundred percent. That happens pretty often, you know. They jack the prices into the stratosphere, compared to what the stuff costs to make."

"Jonah, I've got work to do. You coming home for Thanksgiving? Call your mother and let her know. She'd like that very much."

"I don't know. There's a lot of for-real stuff on that website, Dad. People talk about part-time, contingent, on-demand labor. I've got friends that get their work schedule every week and if they're not needed for the full shift, they're sent home. Others get only a few hours scheduled, then their boss calls them in 'cause there's not enough workers in the store. They get their schedules from corporate once a week, and it always changes. The store manager doesn't even assign the work. It's done by strangers or computer hundreds or thousands of miles away."

"Son, I don't have time . . ."

"People are pissed off, Dad. It's not like when you grew up. The whole corporate-work thing sucks. Hardly anybody gets more than thirty hours a week and it's usually at a non-livable wage. I hear about it all the time. There's an entire gig employment model now prevalent with the younger crowd. How's a person supposed to make it like that? It's what that website, The Anger Express, is all about. Those postings and those videos about the dynamite boxes in the towers outside of Vegas and on the train tracks—those people are heroes! My friends are rooting for them, like crazy. We even talked about it in sociology class. Our professor knew about them, said he emailed Professor Crowder, the one whose idea it was to start the website. Him, and some brainiac student of his. He invited the professor to speak at our college."

"That's fine, Jonah, but I really have to . . ."

"He brought up a point, Dad. You know that the only crime the group has committed is trespassing, and maybe littering."

"They sought to intimidate the government with explosives. They threatened to bomb crucial infrastructure!" Jay's voice was now elevated. "They commandeered a freight train!"

"You mean hitched a ride? Like a hobo who couldn't afford a ticket. I read where the guy in the motorcycle helmet didn't touch the trainman and didn't even have a real gun. They didn't hurt anybody, Dad. They didn't smash up anything."

"It's a federal crime to . . ."

"The engineer gave an interview. Said he was scared at first but after checking out the whole deal said he was happy to be involved. Said if he could, he'd think about doing the same thing on his own."

"Listen, Jonah, and don't interrupt me anymore! It's my job to bring these individuals to justice. You can't have people going around threatening society like that," Jay exclaimed.

"You mean with empty boxes? Standing up for people's rights? Like Doctor King advocating for social change, demanding freedom from corporate injustice backed-up by the government?" Jonah added quietly. "Is that what you mean, Dad?"

"You know what I mean. Listen, I've got to go. Call your mother."

"Okay, I'll probably come for Turkey Day, love you."

"I love you too, son."

Special Agent Carver was looking out the window. Multi-colored autumn leaves were being blown off the trees as he slowly lowered his cellphone and slipped it in his pocket. He didn't notice his partner approaching until Chan was almost at arm's length.

"Got it," Chan said.

"Got what?" Carver's response was slow, distracted.

"The readout on the dynamite manufacturer's chemical trace compound and shipment manifest. Like you asked."

"Oh, yeah, that. What is it?"

"Says here it was shipped to a McKenzie Demolition Company, in Bryan, Texas. That's just outside of College Station, about ninety miles from here."

"McKenzie Demolition?"

"Yes, that's right. You thought of something?" Chan watched as his partner turned toward him, nodding.

"Remember when we checked out that ranch style estate, the one where that website address was registered to?"

"Yes," answered Chan.

"Do you also remember how that young gal wouldn't let us in very far? What was her name? Oh yeah, Susan. I recall seeing a high school rodeo trophy for a Dylan McKenzie. That happened to be the name of one of my instructors back at Quantico. McKenzie."

"McKenzie? The website there was registered to a D. Hendrix," Chan said. "He must've used an alias to purchase the domain name and set up the URL. I should have checked it out." Shaking his head while looking at the ground, the rookie agent offered, "Sorry, sir, I guess I blew it."

"It's okay. Dylan McKenzie, McKenzie Demolition Company and D. Hendrix can't all be coincidences, now can they?" Carver said with a smile. "What did that young gal say her last name was? Susan what?" Carver reached into his pocket and retrieved a small notebook. "Rutherford, Susan Rutherford. Must've been married at a young age and changed her name, that's why we missed it. I suspected she knew something. I'll call Judge Burnett. He'll have a warrant faxed to the car by the time we get there. I say we pay the little lady a visit. What do you think, Kevin? Time for a ride back to the ranch?"

"Yes, sir. I'll get the car."

Dylan, Susan and Brandon were discussing the details of recent events when the two FBI agents pulled up to the main house. Susan let them in the foyer. Carver was the first to speak.

"Good afternoon, Mrs. Rutherford. That's it, right? Susan Rutherford?"

"Yes, that's right. Y'all were here before."

"That's correct, ma'am. We were. But there was some confusion about people's names." With a slight frown, Carver glanced at Chan.

"Evidently, your brother Dylan used a pseudonym establishing his website I.P. address," Chan said.

"A what?"

"A different name," Carver cut in. "But that's not all. The police have listed your property as the location of an unsolved homicide. Our records indicate that this residence is owned by yourself and one Dylan McKenzie. Dylan is your brother. Isn't that right?" Carver said, now looking at Dylan, who had joined them from the kitchen.

"Yes, I'm her brother."

At this point, Julie worked herself up from her chair. Using her walker, she made her way to the group gathered by the front door. Extending one hand while holding onto the walker she smiled and announced, "Hi, I'm Julie. What's this all about? Is the FBI looking for Joe's killer? This whole thing has been absolutely dreadful. I'm so sorry for the two of them."

Carver responded. "I'm afraid not, ma'am. Yet there is a good deal of suspicion raised when someone is killed on the property of a case we're investigating."

"A case you're investigating?" Julie inquired. "What do you mean investigating? What case? Excuse me, will you, I can't stand for very long. I'm afraid my legs aren't what they used to be. You don't mind if I sit back down, do you?"

"That's quite alright, ma'am," Carver said.

Julie turned and, using the walker, went back to her spot on the reclining chair. The group followed her and took seats in the living room.

Carver continued, "We've cross-referenced local employment records and found that a Robert Revere resides here as well. Would that be your husband?"

"Yes, Bob. He goes by Bob. What's he have to do with this?"

"We're not sure, ma'am. Where is your husband now? Is he here?" Carver continued.

"No, he's working. He's a truck driver. He makes deliveries all over the southwestern region. But I guess you know that."

"Where was he the night Joe McKenzie was killed? Was he here?"

"What are you saying? You think my husband killed Joe? Are you crazy? He was out doing his job." Julie shot a desperate glance at Dylan and Susan.

"We don't know. But we do know that the explosive boxes used in two acts of domestic terrorism can be traced back to Joseph McKenzie, the former owner of the McKenzie Demolition Company and the uncle of these two right here. Dylan McKenzie and Susan McKenzie, before she was married and changed her name to Rutherford, that is!"

"I wouldn't call it terrorism," Dylan weighed in. "It's activism—political activism. It's all over my website. There's been more than thirty-five million views of the videos. That's more than ten percent of the population of this country. People are calling the ones that did that stuff heroes."

"Would that be the website you opened as D. Hendrix?" Chan interjected.

"There's nothing wrong with starting a website using a different name. Besides, from what I gather, nobody's been hurt. Nothing's actually been blown up. Isn't that right?"

"As of now, someone has been killed," Carver said in a somber tone. "Your uncle. And it was your uncle's empty explosive containers used in the attacks."

"Attacks? I've seen the videos a dozen times. There were no attacks."

"What about the incident involving the train? Someone held a man against his will and disrupted commerce. If there was nuclear material or U.S. postage on that shipment, there would be a host of additional federal charges. Also, technically, it is an act of fraud to use a false name when purchasing a service. The internet service provider in question could press charges," Chan said, studying Dylan.

Julie and Susan followed the men's conversation. A silent expression of shock cast across their faces.

"Hold on now. What about Joe? You think I killed my uncle too? You people are out of your minds. Anybody could have done those acts of protest. Folks used to ask us for the boxes all the time. Thought they were cool. They'd fill them with road flares and yarn as wicks glued on them. They made displays and gag pieces out of them. Halloween decorations. It's been that way for years. There must be hundreds of those old boxes all over the state of Texas."

"What about Robert Revere? We understand he was unaccounted for the night your uncle was shot. Also there was an RV stolen."

"The cops thought it might have been scumbag meth-heads. They cook crank in motor homes out in the sticks. Drive them out to the middle of nowhere so no one can smell the chemicals. The police think they must have shot our uncle and stole the RV."

"I suppose that's a possibility," Carver said. "But we still would like to talk to Mr. Revere."

"Bob didn't kill anybody! He's not like that! You can't seriously think he shot Joseph, the one who's been more than kind letting us stay here at his ranch." Julie was leaning forward in her chair, one hand on the walker for support. Her words were clipped.

"His ranch?"

"It's our ranch. Susan's and mine," Dylan was quick to answer, shooting a glance toward Susan.

"Listen," Carver said. "We're very sorry about your uncle, and I assure you we'll get to the bottom of this, but until there's a solid connection, our primary focus is determining who's out there setting up these displays of, what did you choose to call it? Protest. Although nobody's been hurt so far and it's been an inconvenience for the electric company and rail line, we're very concerned. The term we use at the Bureau is terrorism, not activism."

"Intelligent people know the difference," Dylan said. "Check the comments on the site. But I'm sure you've already done that, haven't you? Maybe that's why people are—very concerned—as you put it. They should be. It looks like some traction for change is developing, but hey, I just run the site. It's got to be pure coincidence that Uncle Joe's boxes were used."

"I'm sure there is something you could not be aware of," Carver continued, eyes dancing between Dylan and Julie. "In working with the local police, we GPS pinged Mr. Revere's cell phone at the time surrounding the murder of Mr. McKenzie. It shows him being right here on this ranch."

Julie, Dylan and Susan exchanged anxious glances. Nobody spoke.

"We'll let ourselves out. Thank you for your time. We'll contact you when we know more."

THIRTY-TWO

Later that evening after dark, Bob walked in with his bag and found Julie, Susan, Dylan, and Brandon all sitting in the front room of the main house. The mood was somber.

"Last time I made it to Albuquerque on time but I had to wait four hours to unload, due to forklift troubles on the docking bay. This time, they've got me driving a truck so old it's got dinosaur dung stuck in the tire tread. It lacks all the modern upgrades that make a trucker's life bearable, I can't believe it!" He dropped his bag on the floor as he knelt to pet Maggie. "What's going on? You all look like you've seen the ghost of Genghis Khan come collecting for Dracula's blood drive."

Dylan was the first to speak. "We had to tell them, Bob. Well, actually, your wife got most of it out of

Susan, then she figured out the rest." Bob remained silent.

Julie grabbed the handles of her walker and worked herself up to a standing position. She made her way over to Bob. He gave the dog a final pat and rose to meet her. The strained expression on her face couldn't diffuse the natural beauty of the ALS besieged love of his life. Although losing partial ability to control her legs, she continued to arouse a carnal desire in Bob. She lifted her right arm, made a fist, and pounded the heel of her hand into his chest in a forceful stab. "You idiot! What were you thinking? Bombs on railroad bridges. Threatening to blow up electrical towers in the desert. Letters to the government. Are you insane?"

"I did it for you. Those parasites at Physbon Pharma working with the FDA to keep Invigratol off the market until it's approved as a diet aid. They know it's worth billions per year instead of just maybe a million per decade for Lou Gehrig's disease. I couldn't stand it! I had to do something. Jesus Christ, Jules, you're dying because of them. You were young when you joined up. Now they're running a megascam to screw enlistees even more."

Dylan cut in. "It's okay, Bob. We all know why we're doing this, but we've got a bigger problem now. The feds think you killed Joe. They said they pinged your phone and it showed up here. It's a glitch I didn't know about until they mentioned it and I checked it out. Apparently, the GPS zeros on the location where the strip-script software is installed. I've fixed it, but they think you were here."

"Well, that's just great."

"I wondered why they couldn't find you on the road. Doesn't your truck have satellite tracking?"

"Are you kidding? This company is so cheap; they could squeeze two pennies and make it into a dime. These trucks are old school. They rely on paper logbooks and feedback from customers. Nope. No GPS on the rigs I've been driving—although some of the new trucks in the fleet have them. But not mine."

"That's why the feds couldn't ping your truck. You're a murder suspect now, Bob. We have to hide you. You can stay with my buddy down at the Gulf for a while. He can probably use some help anyway. You'll make good money working on the boat, plus keep him company. He can put you up, no problem."

"Wonderful. There goes another job. But Jesus Christ, Dylan, how long am I supposed to hide out? This is nuts! I didn't kill Uncle Joe and you know it."

"We all know it. It's just that it's hard to come up with an alibi that won't land us in a concrete cage when we're out commandeering freight trains in another state."

"Tell me about it."

"By the way, they're probably watching this place. How did you get here anyway? I tried to call you and warn you, but you didn't answer."

"Raul dropped me off at Ken's house, behind you. I owed him money, so I paid him and walked up through the ravine the back way. Also, I realized when I left Tuesday that I forgot my phone in the bedroom drawer. It's probably under a pile of socks."

"Damn good thing you came through the back. That Agent Carver went away with a suspicious mind. I'll think of something. Don't worry."

"Don't worry? I've done nothing but worry since Julie was diagnosed."

"Oh, honey, my brave man. I feel like I'm Bonnie and you're Clyde."

"Clyde is rumored to have been impotent," Brandon chimed in, as he turned to look at Susan, her cheeks now blushing.

"That poor man," was all she could say. A chuckle soon followed. The group was splashed with a much-needed dose of comic relief. Looking back and forth at each other, they all started to laugh.

"You must be tired from the road, Dad," Brandon said. "You want a beer?"

"Does the Pope want peace on Earth?" Bob replied.

Dylan said, "Maybe. But I bet he could use a piece of ass too, same as that poor son of a bitch Clyde." The laughter increased with heads shaking and Susan burying her face in her hands.

"This friend of yours really pays well for catching fish?" Bob said, taking the beer being handed to him by his son.

"Just think of the slimy salt water sloshing around your feet as liquid assets. He can also pay in cash so there's no trace."

"I talked to our insurance company, Bob," Julie said, after taking a healthy chug from her own longneck bottle. "They say we're due an excess of five figures for the stolen motor home."

"That sounds like good news," Bob said, now intently studying the ceiling above his head.

"Why are you looking at the ceiling that way, Dad?"

"I just want to make sure it isn't falling in. Seeing as how almost everything else has been a total slam to my system."

"By the way, and this won't slam your system but it's not the best of news," Julie said. "I got a letter from Lillian Williams today. It seems I'm not the only one going downhill. She is having to find people to help her on her place. She can still feed the chickens and milk the cow, but the harder stuff in the garden, tilling, planting and picking, is just too much for her now."

"From what you've told me over the years, she always was a tough old gal," Bob said. "I remember you telling me she used to work her own chainsaw to clear downed trees on her place."

"That she did. Hey, Brandon, make yourself useful and grab your mom another beer will you, my one and only?"

"Sure, Mom."

*****

Later that evening, after a modest dinner of barbequed chicken and corn on the cob, Dylan rose and announced he was off to check his website. Susan cleared the table and started washing the dishes.

"You know, Bob, I'm having trouble walking, not moaning and groaning," Julie said, just above a whisper with a wry smile.

"Now that you mention it, Jules, I'm a little road weary and could use some sack-time myself." As Bob helped his wife out of the chair, Brandon showed the intuition of a knowing son and fetched them each another longneck.

"Say, Dylan," said Bob, catching him in mid-step, "I've seen evidence of some weapons-grade gray matter concealed in that shaggy-haired knob of yours. I'll slosh around in slimy saltwater for a while, but you better come up with a plan B pronto, or my crystal ball's showing one northern California transplant going postal. If you catch my drift."

"Consider it caught. We're not at DEFCON 5 just yet, you know. We've still got a couple of cards to play. Some on the table and a couple up my sleeve."

THIRTY-THREE

It was almost midnight. Jose Ramirez was piloting the RV stuffed with the explosives liberated from the ranch in Texas when he heard the sound of an incoming text message from the rear sleeping compartment. The men were just outside of Flagstaff. Malach Zelig was up like a scalded cat.

> Operation one-double-X-31
> Update:
> Proceed Phoenix safe house.
> Await further directive.

Although freshly awakened, Malic showed no signs of drowsiness. "Where are we?" he said.

"Approaching Flagstaff. What was the message?"

Malach quickly checked the mapping program on his cellphone. "When you get to Flagstaff, head south on Interstate 17. We're to hole up in the safe house in Phoenix."

"Why? What's the trouble?"

"I don't know. Those are the instructions. We follow orders. That's all."

"Alright. You're the big cheese on this assignment. If I had my way, we'd have waited and laid to rest everybody at that dust pan in Texas. Not just that old hombre by the metal building."

"We only kill when we must, or are told to do so. Don't worry, my friend, I'm sure you'll have ample opportunity to satisfy your bloodlust. I have a feeling this is going to be a big one."

"What makes you say that?"

"You don't think our handlers could have arranged a few high explosives to come our way without having us steal them, along with this rolling monstrosity?"

"You have a point," Ramirez said. "Now that you say it, I always had my materials left at a drop point. Guns, cars, phones, everything."

"Now you see what I'm saying. There is something special about this assignment. Our handlers want us to use these explosives. Not something provided by the company."

"What do you think it is?"

"I don't know. But I don't like it. First we're told to go to San Francisco, and now they're sending us to Phoenix. Either the assignment has changed, or they have us waiting until something else happens. Either way, I don't like it. Now we need to hide this 'recreational vehicle' loaded with dynamite and enough C-4 to level a stadium and stay out of sight ourselves."

Ramirez was silent until he said, "I see the turn coming up, Interstate number 17 south."

Malach was still in the back, phone in his hand, staring out into the obsidian sky. He lay back down. "Wake me when we get to Phoenix. We'll get something to eat and change plates again. We'll give it some time. If we hear nothing after a few days, I'll make some inquiries."

THIRTY-FOUR

The day after going to the McKenzie ranch, Agents Carver and Chan were seated in the Houston FBI office. As before, the image on a large, wall-mounted, flat panel screen was the symbol of their organization and an American flag. Soon the image faded and the words INCOMING CALL and CLASSIFIED bannered across the screen. The grim-faced Sheila Ferguson could now be seen standing behind her desk with a cup of coffee in her hand. A tone was heard and Director Ferguson took a sip from the mug. She set it down, placed both hands on her desk and leaned in closer to the screen.

"I've been monitoring your activities out there in Houston and frankly, I'm not impressed. Agent Carver, you're wearing the daddy-pants on this one. What have you to report?"

"Good morning, Director . . ."

"Can the pleasantries, Agent. The people driving the bus around here want results. Do you have any good news for me this morning or what?"

"Well, ma'am, I believe it's only a matter of time until we get something that's not circumstantial, something solid. If you've been monitoring the case, you know that the explosive containers used in both events track back to the same address as the website listed on the ISP account. That can't be a coincidence. I have a man watching the house, and of course we're monitoring all communications."

"What about that engineer on the train? Perhaps you should speak with him again. Our people here have gone through that thing pixel by pixel. Nothing jumps out as anything but original footage; however, he does seem at the end to be almost enjoying the experience. Maybe you should lean on him some. Enter the notion that unless he comes up with something, we will slap conspiracy charges on him. What do you think?"

"Ma'am, I've seen that video at least a half a dozen times. Agent Chan has run it forward and backward as well. If your forensic team in Washington hasn't come up with anything, I think we need to take it at face value. It is what it is. The engineer was not complicit in the event."

"Don't 'it is, what it is' with me, Agent Carver. I've got orders from the high command that we put this thing to bed this week. It's gone way beyond a social media flash intrigue. Some folks around here are getting more than just a little hot under the collar. This has a serious humiliation factor hitched to it. Some stocks have already taken a hit. You need to put a cork in this bottle of rot gut before some of it splashes on the both of you."

Carver looked at Chan, then back at the screen. "I've been thinking. Maybe we could post a suggestion on the website anonymously. If our suspects take the bait and carry out the action, we'll nail them, especially if they use the same boxes as before."

"I don't care what you do, but you better pull a rabbit out of your hat pretty soon. Believe me when I say we're all in the same boat here."

"Roger that."

"I don't think I need to point out the incendiary nature of this thing. If others get prompted by these crazies, these Pacific Tribal Rioters, if members of the public buy in to the idea that they're some sort of new age patriots and start taking actions on their own, we could have a full-blown rebellion on our hands. You read me, Agents Carver and Chan? You don't want to end up in the history books as the ones who lost control of the good old U. S. of A., do you?"

The two responded in chorus, "No, ma'am."

"Alright then! You boys better put on your thinking caps and come up with a solution." Director Ferguson stepped back and cast a long look at a .45 caliber government-issued Colt 1911. The engraved automatic pistol was visible hanging on the wall behind her desk in a commemorative glass-enclosed frame. She paused for a long moment, studying the display, giving it her full attention. Turning back to the screen without expression she said, "Sometimes things don't go as peacefully as you might like."

"We'll get on it, ma'am. Will that be all?"

She turned back to the screen, "That's all I have. It's up to you, Carver." An icy stare pierced the screen, and Carver felt a jolt of doom take hold of him. For a moment, the nebulous image formed in his mind of the middle-aged, yet somewhat attractive, Sheila Ferguson morphing into a sub-human monster. It gripped him harshly. Carver shook it off. The FBI director leaned forward, lifted an unseen clicker from her desk and the monitor in the Houston office went blank.

Agents Carver and Chan sat in silence. Chan blew out a breath. He looked at Carver. Carver was still staring at the screen before turning to address his partner. "So what do you think of your first genuine assignment out in the real-time world, Kevin? Not all apple dumplings and cherry pie, is it?"

"Did you get that? Jay, come on. The director is getting pretty direct! She wants us to shoot first and ask questions later. Can you believe it? You know, I just thought of something. Since we've been tapping the suspects' phones, the only calls the males have made, or received, have been from anybody except each other."

"Probably using burner phones. Contact the phone company and have them run a data usage scan on all unregistered calls in the area. If we can pin a call or two to an unknown phone at a time and place we know they've been, we might be able to finagle a peephole into their chatter."

"Yes, sir." Chan threw a glance at the office door, reassuring himself that it was still closed. "Anything is better than what the director sugges . . . I mean, well, you know what I mean, right?"

Jay considered his young partner for a moment before responding. "Don't worry, Kevin, my son would never talk to me again if we went assassination squad on their asses. He and his friends follow their antics. Or, I guess I should say, criminal activity. I'd be in the doghouse for sure if we gunned them down without a damned good reason. And right now, I'm fresh out of flea powder."

THIRTY-FIVE

Four days after sending Bob off to the Gulf to hide on his college buddy's fishing boat, Dylan's cell phone rang.

"Dylan, I sure hope your spy-craft software is working."

"It is."

"Things aren't going so well down here. I'm getting seasick like a one-legged hungover deck swab. Plus, this is doing nothing to further the cause. I can't just stay offshore puking my guts out while Julie gets worse. Any change on your end? We've got to come up with something else. Also, I'm not so sure about your buddy Gomez. He keeps asking a lot of questions and his business isn't doing so well. He seems always short of money. How well do you know him anyway?"

"Not all that well actually. We had a couple of classes together my first semester. He seemed alright but I wouldn't tell him too much. You never know. Besides, there's been a change. I'm afraid it's not for the better, I'm sorry to say."

"What's up? Is Julie getting worse?"

"No, it's not like that. We had an answer, of sorts, from The Man."

"Do tell."

"Brandon, Susan, and I were watching the national news. You know, the news-speak-government-mouthpiece out of Washington, when we heard an unusual report."

"Go on."

"It was something to the effect of, 'Upon review of some specialized citizen complaints regarding certain pharmaceutical products submitted to the FDA for approval, the administration has determined to take no action at this time.'"

"Really? No action."

"There's more. The spokesperson said they had considered a number of factors including resource allocation and enforcement priorities, or any procedural FDA violation. They said they were weighing the type and severity of possible consumer injury, or liability on the part of the department."

"No kidding," said Bob, throwing his third cigarette butt of the hour under foot, and twisting it into the concrete surface of the pier.

"They finished by saying that they were advising the consumer group that they would need more time to consider the complaint."

"More time! We're running out of time. No action! Well I'm ready for some action. I'm tired of kissing frogs, Dylan! We need to find the fairy princess pretty soon, or I don't know what to say!"

"We're stuck in a holding pattern, Mr. R. The feds got a handle on our butts, big time."

"I've been thinking of a different approach. Been working out a plan. Not a perfect plan, but a plan anyway."

"You know what they say, a slightly imperfect plan today is better than a perfect plan tomorrow."

"You got it. This social-activism thing is like any other first-time project. Don't let the fact that you don't know what you're doing prevent you from showing up and doing your job."

"You make that up, Bob?"

"Damn right. I'm in construction, remember? A lot of times you don't know what you're going to do until you get into it."

"All right, here's one for you. Confucius say that falcon flying in circles not swooping on field mouse will go hungry. What do you have in mind? Oh yeah, and I did just make that up."

"So far, that car you got me has been flying under the radar. I'm pretty careful also, traveling only at night, getting gas wearing a big floppy hat and shades, and avoiding camera-heavy areas. Plus, since I've had time to think about it, whenever I got my DMV photo taken for the last twenty years, I've had a beard."

"That should help throw off the facial recognition tracking software. I noticed you were clean shaven when I saw you leave a few days ago."

"Yeah, had to tweak my facial features. I'll see you tomorrow night. You still think it's safe to pick you and Brandon up at the neighbor's house behind your place?"

"I'm pretty sure. I've been keeping an eye on those two agents watching the house. So far all they've done is sit their sorry asses in their car down the road and drink coffee."

"Good. Fold up a dozen or so TNT boxes. We'll stick them in the trunk. And get ready for a little trip to the blonde beach-girl state."

"You mean California?"

"That's right. We're going to the museum."

THIRTY-SIX

"Alright, Dad, so what's this brilliant plan of yours?"

"I'll tell you, son, we're going to do an incident that they can't cover up. Something public, a big display."

Dylan was driving and he chimed in, "Can't wait to hear it, boss. What do you have in mind?"

"When I first started dating Brandon's mother, we visited a railroad museum in downtown Sacramento. It's close to the Sacramento River and the train tracks make a curve, just before the river. They run mile-long trains full of nasty, sticky crude oil from the Dakotas, right through town to a plant in Richmond on the San Francisco Bay.

"I'm thinking this time we do a public demonstration. Not something hidden and obscure, like we've been doing."

"We could organize a flash mob. Say we're having a skateboard competition or something maybe," Brandon said.

"Now you're catching on."

"I like it. You know, many train tracks have been there for a hundred years, or more. Major cities developed around the junctures of the trains and rivers. So yeah, there's a lot of them downtown." Dylan flashed one of his mischievous smiles before his expression turned to one of contemplation.

"That's right," said Bob. "And this one just happens to have a train museum. Icing on the cake, I'd say."

"A trifecta of treachery. We get enough people down there with their cell phone cameras having internet access, and the lame-stream media would have to carry the story," said Brandon.

Returning from his thoughtful silence, Dylan spoke up. "That's a great idea. So far we've been restricted from the general public by having our activities only available for view on the website. Even so, we've attracted a strong following. The presstitutes have been squashing the story—I'm sure due to pressure from the government. The big boys can't be too happy they haven't dropped a net on us yet."

"They can suck flaming walrus balls in hell," Bob said, before lighting up a cigarette.

"I'm with you on that one, Mr. R. The internet is the stiff steel spring poking up through the comfy cushion of the ruling oligarchy. The so-called free press is their lapdog these days, pushing their agenda such as wars, a plethora of useless consumer products, and over-priced medications for diseases nobody's ever heard of."

"Damn straight. It's their job to tell the people what to think, wear, drive and eat. What to do. Not at all what the founding fathers had in mind. Well, this time we're going to get them working for us," Bob said.

"It'll be tricky," Dylan said, "doing a stunt in plain view, in the daylight, downtown, in a public area."

"It doesn't fucking matter," Bob said. "Even if it did matter . . . it doesn't matter to me!"

THIRTY-SEVEN

Malach Zelig and Jose Ramirez had been cooling their heels at a Phoenix safe house for almost a week when there was a knock on the door. Malach glanced through the peephole, Uzi in hand, cocked and ready to fire. Jose crouched behind an adjoining wall with both his custom .45 caliber pistols pointed at the ready.

A slim man, fortyish, in a dark suit, looking quite serious, stood on the doorstep. Seeing that the visitor was empty-handed and alone, Malach opened the door with caution. Stepping only halfway through the opening while holding the submachine gun out of sight, he scoured the street with steel cold eyes as he addressed the stranger. "Hello. Can I help you?"

"It's good to finally meet you, Agent Zelig. We've texted may times but never shared the same coordinates. I'm your handler. My name is Bertrand

Jenkins. You can tell Agent Ramirez to stand down. I imagine he's perched somewhere inside with guns drawn as your backup."

Malach stood in silence for a moment. He had never met a so-called 'superior' before. In fact, most, if not all of his operations were done solo. There were times that he thought he'd seen a car leave after dropping off a sniper rifle, some plastique or other necessary tools of the trade. Ramirez was the only partner he'd known thus far and as of yet, they'd only boosted a timeworn RV full of explosives and put an old man out of his misery.

He thought about asking for some form of ID but dismissed the thought as ridiculous. People in his line of work didn't carry employee identification cards. If the man crowding the porch was in law enforcement, Malach knew he'd most likely already be dead. "Won't you come in?" He cocked his head toward the door. Just in case, he kept the Uzi one finger pull from buttonholing his uninvited guest.

"I'll bet you gentlemen must be wondering why we've been keeping you down here, out of circulation."

Jose came up from his place of hiding, first with a look to his partner, then turning to the new arrival, pistols at his sides.

"It's necessary to have you accomplish your mission on a certain date and that date is coming up."

"Then why'd you have us grab the stuff so soon? I don't like sitting around here waiting for the Federales to show up," Ramirez said.

"It was crucial to have you appropriate your supplies the night you did. I've got a surprise for you. We know how much you enjoy the opera, Malach. We've arranged tickets for you and your associate to attend the Phoenix Opera this evening. You have a private balcony booth, naturally. You also have reservations at one of the city's finest restaurants. All expenses courtesy of the Nightshade Group, of course. Cheer up gentlemen; we're giving you the night off. Enjoy yourselves.

"I'm sending someone here to watch the house, and the goodies in the RV."

"Sounds fine to me," said Jose. "I'm tired of eating pizza and ordering in. I'm ready to get this job over with, amigo." He shot another glance at Malach.

Malach, turning from Ramirez, now looked at Bertrand Jenkins. "I agree. This is the longest I've sat on an assignment. Usually it's acquisition, quickly followed by implementation. No lag time."

"This is an important operation. Set to shake things up more than just a little bit. Got to have you boys well-rested, and prepared." The controller answered his phone.

"Just leave the car there and come in. They've been briefed. They'll be ready shortly."

Turning to the two assassins, Jenkins said, "We didn't think you boys would have the appropriate attire for the opera. We're providing you with some formal clothing. We know your sizes, of course."

*****

That night, Zelig and Ramirez dined in style before taking in the opera: Carmen. Small tracking bugs in their suit coats ensured the controller that they stayed where he wanted them to be.

While the men enjoyed the classic performance, a small yet powerful device was placed in a hollow wall of the RV. It was hidden so well that the vehicle could have passed a full DEA Border Patrol inspection with no one being the wiser.

THIRTY-EIGHT

"You know, Bob, people are really responding well to our little stunts of American activism.

I've been monitoring our website. One lady, an experienced trial attorney, posted that officials could be chosen the same way they empanel a jury. Say we needed a new senator, governor, or even a president. Lord knows you don't need any special talent, experience, education or intelligence for the position. Just look at the bonehead that got us into the Middle Eastern wars.

"She says you could simply send letters to regular citizens. People not wanting the position could opt out. You establish equal campaign funding for all participants, provided by the government. No special interest money. The contenders then run their campaigns, stating their qualifications and strengths. In the end, the people vote, same as now. In this way, you eliminate the sociopaths drawn to positions of power and the influence of big money in politics."

"You'd still get sociopaths, Dylan," said Bob.

"I know. But it would be random sociopaths. Not calculating ones like career politicians out to enrich themselves and their contributors. Besides, after seeing the candidates and hearing their pitch, the people would still decide by voting."

"You're right," Brandon chimed in. "Money buys the votes these days."

"Not to change the subject . . . except I am," said Bob. "But I've been thinking about our next act of protest. Dylan, this might cost a few thousand."

"We're cool, Mr. R. I've got the credit card numbers liberated from the banksters by way of high-tech pilferage. And let's not forget, we've got to make Uncle Joe proud, while avenging his death."

"All right, here's the deal. I say we buy a few dozen frozen turkeys and raffle them off at our skateboarding competition at the railroad museum in downtown Sacramento. We can hire people off the internet to do it all. We get homeless people to hand out the turkeys. They'll get one hundred dollars each for their service.

"We say this is to bring attention to the plight of the homeless in this country. We phone in the announcement to radio stations and post it on social media."

"This is sounding good, Dad. It is the beginning of November. People will be starting to think about Turkey Day."

"That's right. Thanksgiving is coming up. Some people have plenty to be thankful for. Many do not."

"What do we say when asked who's sponsoring the event?" Dylan inquired.

"We say it is a group of concerned individuals to be revealed at the skateboard exhibition," said Bob.

"You mean . . . "

"Of course! The Pacific Tribal Rioters."

"We'll be up close and personal with people," said Brandon. "How are we supposed to disguise ourselves and not get caught?"

"Again, it's all done anonymously with prepaid cards and drop points. Once the so-called leading co-ordinators, hired from job posting sites, are confident they'll get paid, they'll do what we want."

"And then?" said Dylan.

"After a sizeable crowd has gathered and all the turkeys have been given out, we park a flatbed truck on the tracks with our empty boxes of explosives strapped on the back. While the winners are being announced, we remove the tarp and have something that distributes leaflets saying that there are two types of turkeys in existence. The kind you can eat and the hidden kind that keeps people impoverished, sick and serving a merciless taskmaster. You know, the government-enabled corp-rat structure."

"Mr. R., I can rig up a small charge from an auto airbag out of a junk yard that will disburse flyers while attracting attention for sure. Of course, this does go against my no-litter policy, but that's been tossed ever since we started this gig. I guess it's true what they say, you can't make a good country album without a few broken heart songs."

"Yes! And when it is revealed that our TNT boxes are empty, it will be obvious that a bigger boom would cause catastrophic, devastating havoc, if real explosives blew as a train came down the tracks."

"Damn right," Brandon cut in. "Major shipping companies, coal-fired power plants, chemical companies and oil refineries all rely on rail service, not to mention passenger and even nuclear materials transportation. Just like that FBI guy said."

"Many communities are already concerned about trains full of toxins passing through their city. Imagine the horror raised about a trainload of deadly chemicals or oil, dumped into the main river of a capital city that flows into the San Francisco Bay?"

"Yeah, and right in front of the train museum. I love it," Dylan said grinning.

"You know who will really take notice is the insurance companies. How many millions of dollars would have to be paid off after a mile-long train of toxic sludge splattered downtown in a disaster like we're demonstrating?" Brandon said.

"It shouldn't be hard to draw a crowd. People are hurting. Almost a third of all millennials, those aged 25-34, live with their parents," Dylan said.

"No kidding . . . " Bob said, with a quick glance at his son.

"Hey, hold on a minute, Pops. You're living with me. I'm not living with you, remember?"

"Yeah, I know, that makes it even worse."

"The dying middle class is no longer a majority, yet it supports both the rich and the poor. Soon, we'll resemble some South American countries, having a ruling elite and a bunch of serfs."

"There are only two political parties. The rich—influencing the feds, either alone or as organized groups—and everybody else," Dylan interjected.

"CEOs making four hundred times the average person's salary. Private companies charging job applicants for examinations with no guarantee they'll ever get hired. Nowadays you need a special cooking-temperature compliance certificate just to get a job flipping burgers."

"Make a law, make a business," Dylan said. "You're talking about the nation as a whole. Spelled H-O-L-E. A deep pit devouring the sweat energy produced by those who can actually get hired and remain employed. Payday advances, car-title loans, tow truck drivers buying car-loan default information to repo cars. GPS devices shutting down vehicles when people miss a car payment. Lost homes and shattered dreams. The list goes on and on."

"How about the fact that EBT cards are now accepted almost everywhere," Brandon continued.

"Yeah, that's a good one. The corp-rat conspirators have figured out that the EBT card, what was known as food stamps, is the 'new money'," Dylan said.

"You're right," Bob said. "I've seen 'EBT accepted' signs in smoke shops. Don't they have to actually sell food or something?"

"They sell a small amount just to be compliant," Dylan said.

"Well, we shouldn't have any trouble getting people to our free event," Bob said. "Maybe we can have a theme name for it. EBT Day. Every Body gets a Turkey, Day."

THIRTY-NINE

Seventy-five-year-old Dr. Wong had failing eyesight. This was made worse by driving at night. If he hadn't stayed late at the clinic, he wouldn't be driving now on a steep street in downtown San Francisco.

Kanesha Jones didn't like being in an unfamiliar part of the city pushing her baby stroller after dusk. Not wishing to go all the way to the intersection, she was crossing in the middle of the block when she got the text.

Kanesha's sister was informing her that her landlord wouldn't accept her as a tenant. The mother and her baby had been ousted from her low-rent apartment due to a new building being built on the site. In her despair, she almost dropped her phone while crossing Powel Street.

She was quick to snatch her phone out of thin air before it hit the ground. In doing so, she lost control of the stroller and fell face first on the pavement.

The pink stroller, now careening unattended on a collision course directly in front of Dr. Wong, forced a reflex action. Jerking the wheel, he avoided the infant. His shiny new SUV, now out of control, ran over a green electrical junction box protruding from the sidewalk before slamming into a storefront. The baby stroller stopped by itself at the curb.

*****

Patricia Alverez was unaccustomed to working at night. She did, however, feel lucky to be employed by the Bay Area Rapid Transit system, known locally as BART. After being on the job for only a few weeks, she had undergone most of her training in the east bay. Thus far, her color blindness had been a well-kept secret.

She repaired the severed com-lines controlling the Powel Street cable car to the BART relay system. In doing so, she accidently attached an older, unused, wire to the new upgraded system. Her shift foreman confirmed that the day crew would install a new terminal box in the morning. After running a final check, she repositioned the damaged green metal cover over the hole in the sidewalk. She wrapped caution tape around the box smashed by Dr. Wong and set orange cones on either side.

*****

Malach and José were relieved to be out of the Phoenix safe house and almost to a private garage in the City by the Bay.

"Hey, amigo, find me a spot to drain the main vein. These beers got my back teeth floating. The toilet on this rig is full of TNT, I can't piss in there."

"I'll pull into this parking lot up ahead. Make it quick and don't be seen. There, just go behind that van and hurry up!"

They entered the commuter parking lot adjacent to the BART station. At 1:02 A.M., they passed under the security camera mounted high on a pole overlooking the lot.

The hotel clock radio in Houston registered 3:42 A.M. FBI Agent Carver was awakened by his cell phone, buzzing its way across the hotel nightstand.

With eyes pasted half-shut, he answered the call. "Hello."

"A charter boat fisherman, one Captain Gomez in southern Texas, called about a reward offered on your suspect after seeing a notice on TV. Evidently the man was staying with him for a few days but now he's gone. Also, we got a hit on that RV allegedly stolen from your suspect's location. It popped up in San Francisco. Our people there have been notified. I've booked you and Chan on the next flight out. You better get down to the airport—like now, Inspector."

Director Ferguson, not waiting for a reply, continued, "Agent Chan should be meeting up with you in about ten minutes."

Carver, still trying without success to scrape the cobwebs out of his brain, responded, "Yes, ma'am. Are there any other new developments?"

"As a matter of fact, yes. A couple of TV stations out of Sacramento ran a story on the eleven o'clock news. It seems some do-gooders were passing out frozen turkeys by a railroad museum at the waterfront. When the turkeys had been dispersed, a small explosion alerted people to a truck full of empty dynamite boxes parked on the tracks. The blast blew some boxes off the truck and it blew hundreds of notices into the air. Nobody was hurt, but the notices were directing people to support your quarry."

"You mean the Pacif . . . "

"Yes, Carver. The Pacific Tribal pain in the asses! We can't keep a lid on this situation any longer. The story is spreading. We're trying to keep it off the morning national news, but not all the networks are in the loop. We can't control every station.

"You two better get out there and bring a hammer down on these clowns. It'll be all of our butts in a sling if you don't. You understand?"

"Got it. Anything else?"

Carver heard a dial tone. The message on his small phone screen read 'call ended.'

Carver tossed the phone on the nightstand with a disparaged look at his pillow. There was a knock on the door. "All right I'm coming," he mumbled aloud. In a hushed voice he said to himself, "Son of a bitch! . . . Yeah, I'm coming."

The pounding on the steel roll-up door sounded like the authorities conducting a raid on Al Capone's whiskey warehouse. Malach tensed. At the same time, he received a text from Bertrand Jenkins commanding him to open up. With his Uzi in one hand, he unhooked the chain and raised the door with the other.

"Good morning, gentlemen," Jenkins said with a smile. He handed each man a large coffee and passed a bag containing two fresh bagels to Ramirez.

Malach, still holding the Uzi he'd grabbed from beside his cot, pointed the weapon at the controller's head as Jose closed the roll-up door. "Alright, Jenkins, or whatever your real name is, enough of this crap! You better come clean with us right now or I'll splatter your brains all over the wall and set off this load of sparklers just for fun." With a nod to Jose, he continued. "We both have enough money stashed to walk away from this bullshit forever."

"Calm down, Agent. I'd heard you Israelis had a temper but today is the big day, gentlemen. It'll make taking out the twin towers in New York City look like some lame kid knocking down sandcastles. Today we're going for the big enchilada. You're going to pop the cork on that washed-out camper in the middle of the Golden Gate Bridge."

"I was wondering what the ram air parachutes were for," Malach said, still holding the nine-millimeter Uzi to Jenkin's forehead.

"That's right," Jenkins continued. "We'll have a boat waiting for you on the Marin County side. A blue and white cigarette speedboat. You'll be delivered to a waiting car, with an excellent driver. Then a private jet will take you to a well-deserved vacation in Ecuador."

"Ecuador, pinche carron!" Ramirez cursed, spitting on the floor. "How about Brazil? I like the beaches, the senoritas."

"From Ecuador, you can go anywhere you like."

Jenkins used two fingers with a slow motion, eyes locked on Malach, and eased the business end of the submachine gun down away from his face.

"There's just one little thing we need to do first," the Nightshade leader continued. "Jose, you'll be taking a car across to the Marin side to pick up another camper full of explosives."

"What? What about this one? This one's loaded."

"Yes, but since this maneuver was first planned, the locals installed a zipper on the bridge."

Malach and Jose glanced at each other. The men almost in unison started to lower their gazes down to their own zippers—catching themselves in the act, their heads bounced up and shot a cold stare at Jenkins.

"A zipper," the controller continued. "A movable concrete barrier lengthwise down the center of the span. A specially designed truck goes along moving the barrier one lane to the right or left, depending on traffic flow. It's like those old toy snakes. A bunch of segments connected by steel links. Except these are concrete blocks."

"Oh, I see. To prevent the head-on collision?" Ramirez said.

"That's right. That's why we need two vehicles. One from each direction parked by the support cables. Then you boys jump, count to three and press your remotes to blow the sucker in half."

C arver and Chan checked into the San Francisco FBI office to plan their strategy. All they knew was that a stolen RV that had gone ghost in Texas had now reappeared in the City by the Bay.

There was no way one could drive that many miles without passing dozens of cameras. These cameras not only scanned license plates but through high-tech computer algorithms detected modifications such as special racks, lights, and dents, or other damage: anything punched into the system.

Of course Odin, being at the top of the pyramid compared to the meager FBI interstate camera software, had implanted a blind spot in the tracking code for this certain RV. Odin, however omnipotent it may be, and designed to run on the latest high-speed networks, had been outdone by a greenhorn technician reconnecting cable car and BART transfer relays one night, by accident, to the older system.

Doing police work the old-fashioned way, Special Agents Carver and Chan proceeded to the downtown BART station that had first detected their prey to interview anyone who might have seen the vehicle and to gather whatever information they could.

One paraglider parachute and one remote control were transferred from the Reveres' appropriated RV to a car provided by Jenkins. Ramirez was given instructions, directions and a strict timetable. He was also told there would be a waterskiing life vest waiting for him in the other RV, parked discreetly off the road on the Marin County side of the bridge. Jenkins retrieved a water-ski vest from his car and handed it to Malach. Before Ramirez took off, the three men studied the details. Timing was of the essence.

*****

Having reached the RV on the northern side of the Bridge, Ramirez called Malach, as instructed. Both men readied themselves by donning the ram air para-chutes over their water-ski vests.

The two assassins placed identical remote controls in their upper pockets. Ramirez looked at the stacked boxes of explosives that filled his RV. He pulled the remote out of his pocket for one last look to make sure it was in the full safe mode. He didn't need it going off if he accidentally brushed against it as he scratched his ear or adjusted his seat belt. With great care, the device was returned to his pocket. Using his forearm, he wiped the sweat from his brow.

They checked their watches. Zero hour at mid-span was eleven o'clock. Routes, traffic patterns, and possible delays had been studied carefully. If they drove at normal speed, they would reach the center of the bridge at the same time. Being in constant cell phone contact ensured that each driver could adjust his speed to accomplish this goal. They each were roughly twenty minutes away from the detonation point.

*****

With an APB being out on Bob and Julie's pilfered RV, reports had come in from various points around the city. One quite promising report was of the mo-torhome in question being spotted at the San Francisco National Cemetery, one of only four ceme-teries in the city limits. This beautiful location overlooks the bay and is in the crux of the two major freeways leading to the Golden Gate Bridge. Having followed up another false lead and not finding the stolen RV, Carver turned to Chan and said, "Not there either. I'll tell you one thing though; I sure could stay a while, just to take in the view."

"No kidding. That place had a view to die for."

Carver looked at his partner. "What, are you trying to be funny?" Chan sank down in his seat, his face turning a shade of pale red.

"No, sorry, sir. It just kind of slipped out."

"I guess we'll head back to the office, see if anything new has turned up." Carver's GPS led him onto the 101 Freeway, roughly one mile from the toll plaza of the Golden Gate Bridge. He was heading east, away from the bridge toward downtown.

Chan shot up in his seat. "Hey, what the—look at that!"

By bizarre chance, the two FBI agents had just been passed by the target of their search going in the opposite direction in the fast lane. Carver, with lightning quick reflexes, caught a good glimpse of the driver of the RV. Passing within six feet of each other, in spitting range, on a bright morning, it was apparent that the driver was anyone but their suspect. The driver of the RV was an older, balding, olive-skinned man—clearly not Robert James Revere.

"I can't believe it! There it is! Chan, call it in! Tell HQ that they're headed for Marin County." As Chan took out his phone, the two men looked at each other. In what seemed like simultaneous slow motion they each vocalized their next thought.

"He's going across the Golden Gate Bridge!"

With the short concrete safety wall separating the north and southbound lanes of highway 101, there was no way Carver could turn around. He proceeded to the next exit, departed the freeway, and got back on in the opposite direction.

Chan called in the sighting. The agents knew that the RV would have passed the tollgate by the time the bridge authorities got the call. Carver pulled the magnetic cherry out of its compartment, placed it on top of the sedan and hit the siren. Cars began to shuffle to the side as the red light flashed while he and Chan gave pursuit.

*****

Every nerve in Malach's body felt spring loaded. The gravity of his current assignment couldn't be denied. Had he ever killed this many people before with a single act? No. Of course not. Like Jenkins had said, this was the big enchilada. Funny that Ramirez hadn't said that. His contemplation was displaced by Ramirez on the phone.

"I'm on the causeway. Heading to the first tower."

"I'm just past the toll gate on the bridge now."

"Rodger that, amigo. I see what that asshole meant about the zipper. I can see it now, coming my way. Nothing like this in my country."

"Never mind, I'll see you in the middle."

"Here I come." Ramirez began to sing as he piloted his vehicle with the full knowledge he was about to kill hundreds of people, forever alter the lives of thousands, and ultimately disrupt the lives of millions. "London Bridge is falling down, falling down, falling down. London Bridge is falling down, my fair lady…"

"Shut up and proceed," Malach barked. Unable to locate the pocket at his side, he threw the phone on the floor.

The two RVs slowed as they approached the spot where the massive support cables slung down to their lowest point, close to the blacktop on the bridge. Motorists were honking their horns. Some made obscene gestures while passing the stalled recreational vehicles. Jose Ramirez exited his driver's side door and pulled the two .45 caliber pistols out, lowering them at traffic coming his way. Traffic stopped. The zipper truck was almost upon him when the driver slowed to a standstill. He didn't see the weapons as Ramirez had his back to the driver.

"Hey man, what do you think you're doing? You can't stop there," he said, looking down from the cab of the utility truck.

Turning to face the truck driver, and with double shot precision, Jose pumped two rounds into the man's chest. Now smiling to himself, he casually walked across his side of the bridge and jumped the barricade to meet his partner on the other side. Malach, now out of his RV, had his weapon drawn facing the slowing traffic heading north.

*****

"Holy Mother of Christ! What the hell's going on? We'll never get there in time!" shouted Carver. Traffic was slowing to a crawl on the northbound side of the bridge. Now some thousand feet past the tollgate, he threw the door open, jumped out and started to run toward the commotion at the center of the span.

Emergency lights and sirens came on all along the famous structure. Cars were stopped ahead as a panicked crowd rushed toward him and Chan. He produced his FBI badge, but it did little, except to warn those closest to give him a slightly wider berth.

*****

Jose, having reached the other side of the bridge and now standing beside Malach, looked in the water far below. "There it is! That must be it!" He was pointing to a blue and white cigarette-style speedboat floating just off the pylon of the north tower. "There's our escape boat just like Jenkins said."

He looked at Malach, who was already pulling the remote from his pocket and releasing the first safety switch on the device. Ramirez did the same. The two men climbed the handrail. Ramirez looked at the crowd that was now figuring out this wasn't just some stupid sophomoric stunt. He blew them a kiss good-bye and jumped, followed by his partner.

*****

Bertrand Jenkins, binoculars in hand, stood high on a hill of the Marin headlands. Reassured that everything was going to plan, and having unseated the primary safety switch on his remote control when the two RVs stopped and parked in the middle of the bridge, he saw the men jump. With no intention of counting to one—let alone three—he pushed the button.

*****

The tourist couple from New Zealand were pleased as punch they had won a sightseeing speed-boat cruise on a chartered boat in the San Francisco Bay. Such a pretty blue and white cigarette boat it was too, now bobbing in the shade of the north tower. Maddie jumped back in her seat, practically falling over. She was just pointing out to Roy two oddly dressed figures, high up on the bridge, leaping into the clear November sky when the powerful explosion obliterated the jumpers and the center of the mighty steel structure. Roy almost dropped his Pina Colada. The heat from the blast blew over them like a wildfire during a mid-summer Australian windstorm. Cars, trucks, shredded orange metal, strands of cable flying like spinning bolas, and human bodies were dropping everywhere.

Part Three

9-11 2.0 End Run – Second to None

The two towers had withstood the blast. The people of San Francisco couldn't believe it. The Golden Gate Bridge had been blown in half!

The connecting surfaces leading to the towers from the mainland of Marin County and San Francisco also remained. An unnatural balancing act occurred between the causeways leading to the towers and the length of roadway extending into the gaping void. The sections protruding toward the former center span hung in abhorrent fashion. Their torn support cables were infused with various pieces of the adored structure. They dangled in a horrific display, reminiscent of twisted orange tinsel engulfing mangled toy cars.

News helicopters kept the mandated distance of two miles away, established by the authorities within minutes of the blast. Their telephoto cameras conveyed a relentless stream of video imagery to a global audience of transfixed voyeurs.

Surrounding the pandemonium, Coast Guard helicopters searched the bay for survivors. Sheriffs' helicopters and boats combed the shoreline of Marin County where the bridge connected to its base. Also SFPD helicopters and drones circled in similar search and rescue mode above the city waterfront.

San Francisco International Airport, Oakland, all local airports, and unaided landing strips were shut down. Only pre-authorized law enforcement, D.O.T., military, or other official aircraft, were allowed access. Coast Guard vessels and smaller Navy boats patrolled the cold waters of San Francisco Bay. Huge cargo vessels as well as all marine activity was mandated to stay five miles offshore or had been directed to another port. Those already inside the Bay were held at their docks until further notice, inspection, and release.

Assorted cars, trucks, vans, and delivery vehicles were backed up from the chaos in their respective lanes. Some, although damaged, or having their windshields blown out and the occupants peppered with flying glass, attempted to turn around. Many had fallen into the bay or were destroyed in the explosion. A few had been hurled far from the detonation site with the powerful force of the blast. Others were either enmeshed in the supporting cables of the magnificent structure, or were gradually slipping toward an aquatic abyss far below.

People screamed, crawled, or ran, wounded or physically unharmed. Some helped the injured; many videotaped the wicked event with cell phones. The most photographed manmade structure in the world was getting photographed now like never before.

Others stared blankly, shocked into immobility at the horrific scene. Some, on the remaining sections of the blacktop, were pointing and waving their arms. Their efforts being a desperate attempt to direct rescue vessels to the few frantic souls splashing below in a futile attempt to cheat the liquid death that would soon overpower the adrenaline coursing through their shivering bodies.

There were also military helicopters, gunships, and twin-rotor troop transport vehicles hovering in an ominous fashion or circling in small patterns above the population centers.

This time, the reaction to a West Coast 9-11 was not firefighters and other first responders rushing to help the victims of a tragedy, although this was unfolding on the scene. This time the response was an unsettling display of military presence.

Sunday in Sacramento had gone off without a hitch. A few homeless people handed out turkeys to folks holding winning tickets under the watchful eyes of two managers hired from a job search website—role-playing as benevolent contest organizers. Everyone was paid in cash by a well-disguised Dylan, including the owner of a used flatbed truck. When the truck, driven by an equally well-disguised Brandon onto the train tracks, blew its airbag charge sending hundreds of leaflets into the air, the media took notice and the event made the local news. The Pacific Tribal Rioters were now a subject of discussion and debate coupled with suspicion, but there was no denying they were getting plenty of airplay.

*****

The trio left the roadside motel before check out time. They had celebrated their newly earned importance late into the evening with a few stiff drinks. After agreeing to drive a while, allowing their systems to reset from hangover to hunger, they piled into the sedan Dylan had secured for Bob. Not wanting to hear any annoying commercials on the radio, they left Sacramento listening to CDs and smartphone-recorded music.

*****

Bob's cellphone rang. "What the hell's going on?" Julie asked. "What did you do? Where are you? Where's Brandon? What the fuck is going on, Bob?"

"Hold on a sec. What do you mean? You knew what we were going to do."

"Yeah, right," she said. "You never told me you were going to blow the Golden Gate Bridge in half!"

"What?"

"You heard me. It's all over the news. They're saying you and your little group blew up the Golden Gate Bridge." She switched the screen on her phone to FaceTime with the speaker on, and held it so Bob could see the TV behind her. She then turned it back to herself.

"Holy Christ!" Bob looked into the screen at Julie.

Her exquisite hazel eyes now penetrated his soul like a laser. "You really did it this time, Bob."

"Let me see that." Dylan grabbed the phone out of Bob's hand. "I can't believe it. She's right. And they're blaming it on us."

Brandon pulled Dylan's arm so he could get a view. "I'll be damned."

Dylan reached for his laptop. Throwing it open, he began punching buttons. Within seconds, a New York TV station showed helicopters flying around the remains of the pride of San Francisco, still disgorging its automotive contents into the bay.

Bob grabbed the phone from Brandon. "Give me that. Look, honey, we didn't do it. We're just now getting out of Sacramento, I swear."

Dylan showed Bob a picture of himself on his laptop. The banner read FBI seeking Mastermind Domestic Terrorist Robert James Revere. Bob's jaw dropped. He mouthed the word 'What?' and shot a glance at Dylan. "Julie, hold on. I've got to see this. Here, talk to Brandon." He handed the phone to his son.

"Don't worry they can't track us. I installed my strip-script program on her and Susan's phones before we left," said Dylan. "We should be alright . . . for now."

Brandon drove, allowing the other two to share the back seat and monitor Dylan's satellite-enabled laptop. The story continued, now stating, "A traitorous group of domestic terrorists, known as the Pacific Tribal Rioters—who sought to destroy the power grid and intercontinental rail system—have now succeeded in blowing up the Golden Gate Bridge."

Before the trio could stop for lunch, the president made a short announcement.

"The wave of violence in this country has reached tsunami proportions. This cannot be allowed. This evening I will be meeting with members of Congress and a team of legal experts, and tomorrow I will sign new legislation designed to curb the epic plague that has taken hold of this country."

"I wonder what he's talking about?" said Brandon over his shoulder.

"I don't know," replied Dylan, "but one thing's for sure, they high-jacked our scheme for their own twisted agenda. We're being Oswalded!"

"What do you mean?" asked Bob.

"Check it out, dude. Somehow we played right into their hand. We didn't blow the bridge, either of them. We didn't put Vegas in the dark. They're hanging this catastrophe on us, our actions. It's a false flag."

"False flag?" Bob asked.

"Yeah, false flag. You know, when you identify yourself as the good guys, then later show your true colors. According to these reports they're already calling it another 9-11, since it was shrewdly done on the reverse of the numbers themselves. Eleventh month, ninth day!"

"Many believe the real 9-11 was a false flag event designed to get us into the Middle East wars. Hell, people say the plans to invade Iraq and six other countries had been drawn up years beforehand. By the way, it wasn't a bunch of turban-headed jokers running around in sandals who came to America and jacked a couple of airliners."

"Who was it then?"

"Think about it. Who stands to gain by having the mighty U.S.A. attack all of their neighbors? Who has already taken territory? Who's our so-called ally in the region?"

"You mean Isra ..."

"Now you're catching on! Not to slam the Jewish people, I'm talking about the nation-state itself. It has nothing to do with religious zealots, which is just a smoke screen. It was the deep state, or more likely, a deep-seated splinter group led by former members of the Mossad or other rouge entities loyal to that small country with a 'new world order' obsession festering in their minds. They're the remora, leading the shark—the United States. It's been that way for a long time. Many highly placed people in government, banking, business, and the entertainment industry hold dual U.S./Israeli citizenship. It had to be a coordinated action, at the highest levels. No doubt about it.

"There's a conglomerate of engineers, architects, explosives experts, metallurgists, etc. called the '9-11 Truthers' disputing the official story. You can look it up yourself. Also, there were actually three buildings that came down that day. World Trade Center Number Seven—another steel structure 500 feet tall collapsed about 5:30 P.M. This was supposedly done by flying debris causing fires to melt structural columns. What a bunch'a jive! Not to mention people there, at the time, hearing explosions and the three buildings pancaking in free fall, just the way they did

when Uncle Joe and I dropped them doing profes-
sional demolition work."

"Are you kidding? I never heard that."

"Most people didn't. Americans are taught to believe what their institutions tell them, even if they
might question otherwise. Some think Roosevelt
knew about the attack on Pearl Harbor, yet let it occur
to get the people behind entering the Second World
War. Did you know that our aircraft carriers just happened to be out at sea that morning? It's easier to
believe a lie, than accept the truth."

"I never figured you for a conspiracy guy, Dylan."

"Hey, that's the handle they slap on those who
think beyond the lockbox. We pessimists—we're just
better informed. But now I'm wondering what they
really have in mind. We've been set up, and you can
bet your ass it's for some good reason. On second
thought, I'll rephrase. I doubt there's anything good
about it at all."

Bob's phone rang. He clicked it on speakerphone.
"Yes, dear, sorry if I seemed rude before but Dylan
and I are trying to figure out what to do. I duck every
time a car passes. I hide my face each time we go under an overpass, or anywhere there might be a camera.
I'm afraid the whole world is looking for me. It's just
lucky I've had a beard for so long. I guess that's the
only picture they have, my driver's license photo
from California. I shaved. Remember the last time

you saw me clean-shaven? Brandon was in grade school."

"Bob, listen. In all the confusion, I forgot to tell you. Two things actually. One, I received a letter stating I'm being accepted into the drug study program for Invigratol. It says they want to increase the participants to ensure a higher degree of accuracy."

"That's great, Julie. Brandon, did you hear that?

"That's great, Mom!" Brandon shouted over his shoulder. "I love you, Mom."

"Hold on, there's more. Remember Lillian Williams, the lady I knew when I was a little girl? We've been pen pals, most of my life. I invited her to our wedding, but she couldn't leave her chickens and her cow."

"Yes, I remember."

"Well, I got another letter. This one from an attorney's office in Steamboat Wells. Lillian lived just outside of the White River National Forest. That's Northwest Colorado, Bob, it's beautiful there."

"Yeah, okay, attorney's office?"

"That's right. I'm afraid . . . " there was a pause through muffled sobs and Julie continued, "I'm afraid she passed on, Bob."

"Oh, honey, I'm so sorry to hear that. I know you loved her like a second mother."

"And she always loved me too, like the daughter she never had."

"I know, Julie, I'm so sorry"

"But that's not it, Bob. She left me her property. We've inherited ninety-two acres in the Colorado wilderness."

The trio of fugitives drove the remainder of the day and well into the night as far away from California as they could. After spending the evening at the most no-tell hotel they could find, and smuggling Bob in and out, they resumed their way back to Texas. The radio news covered little else other than the disaster now being called 9-11 2.0.

A big part of the story was the fact that within minutes of the disaster, heavily armed SWAT style police, sheriff, National Guard, Homeland Security, and military formations were stationed in strategic downtown locations nationwide. It seemed an almost instantaneous deployment of half-tracks, small tanks, command-center trucks, and personnel transport vehicles in an unmistakable display of paramilitary force. The official line being this was precautionary positioning in case the rebel saboteurs planned multiple strikes in major U.S. cities.

"Check this out, guys," said Dylan highlighting a section of his laptop. "Are they going to shut down the country? You remember the Boston marathon attacks? They shut down a huge area of the city affecting millions of people for hours, just to find two guys. I recall wondering if it was a test to see how long urbanites would endure martial law."

"Yeah, I remember," said Bob. "And that was only two guys with backpacks. Look what they're doing now, coast to coast. Rolling out the big show. Intimidation to any and all who may oppose. They're definitely flashing a bulging jockstrap. And you know when that manly Freudian, stiff-barreled potential is aroused, it doesn't like to be put away without firing a shot or two."

"You really have a colorful way of putting it, Dad."

"Yeah, Mr. R., but it's true. They set up a national defense front in record time. I'm thinking it looks like they were ready in advance. You can't disperse that amount of equipment and manpower that quickly without prior coordination or warning."

"You're right," Brandon said. "It's like prohibition, or when they declared a national 55 MPH speed limit. It's the feds rising up. Telling everybody what to do, or what not to do."

"Yeah, but this time there's armed forces in the streets. They sure as hell didn't do that when they shut off the booze and set a new traffic law."

*****

As was promised, the president made an announcement.

"My fellow citizens. I have met with a special session of Congress. The violence in this country has reached epic proportions. This cannot be denied. It has clearly been shown that an outlaw band of domestic terrorists can do immeasurable harm to our vital systems of transportation and energy. This group calling itself The Pacific Tribal Rioters is responsible for innumerable deaths and indescribable disruption for thousands of people in the great city of San Francisco, and the Bay Area. Not to mention decimating a beloved national treasure.

"Fortunately, other disasters planned by this group in weeks prior have been averted by the swift action of law enforcement. I am speaking of an attempt to blow up high-voltage power lines in the Nevada desert, potentially crippling the city of Las Vegas. And an attempt to blow up a bridge in Colorado that would have distressed commerce and sent millions of dollars' worth of consumer goods, railroad equipment, and masses of toxic substances to the bottom of the river."

"That's a bunch of B.S.," Dylan said. "They never stopped us. We didn't actually attempt any of that stuff. We only demonstrated that we could."

"Quiet," Bob said. "I want to hear what he has to say."

The president continued, "In an effort to quell this national plague of unrestrained violence upon our citizenry, I have mandated strict firearms laws at a federal level. These will take effect as of 12:00 midnight Friday, three days from now. At that time it will be a federal offence to transport any firearm in public without obtaining a permit from the ATF, available on its website. All concealed carry permits are now void—being subject to review. Certain concealed carry permits may be allowed if a recognizable need can be proven. Also, in the coming months, all firearms, including antiques and curios, must be registered with the ATF. In conjunction with this, all firearms must be stored in an approved secure location."

"What the . . . "

"Quiet, Dylan."

"Firearm storage will be allowed at federally-certified armories, permitted gun and rifle ranges, as well as selected police and sheriff's departments. Certified law enforcement and specified military personnel are exempt, requiring a review every two years.

"Other restrictions will be mandated as well. You can find out more by going to the ATF website. Gun owners currently in the system will receive letters, texts, and emails informing them of these new statutes. Those who possess unregistered firearms have thirty days to comply, and either register or relinquish their weapons. Persons found being out of compliance face a potential five-year federal prison term and up to a $250,000 fine per weapon."

"There it is," said Dylan. "The last speck of what you thought was freedom just got whooshed away like a dandelion in a hurricane."

"What do you mean?" Brandon asked.

"Christ, Brandon, don't you see? If the government has all the guns, the people are defenseless. You remember the Nazis, Pol Pot, and Edie Amin? Dictators who murdered millions of their own people after confiscating the guns. If the people can't resist an oppressive government, they are not citizens. They are subjects."

"That's right," said Bob, "gun control isn't about guns—it's about control."

"Yeah, and now they pulled a false flag maneuver second only to the original 9-11 and they're blaming us," Brandon said. "And according the president's speech, it looks like they did an end run around the Second Amendment."

"Wait 'till they hit cruising altitude, dude, then they can run the table placing tighter restrictions on everything concerning guns. We're screwed."

After some thought, Dylan said, "I think this might not be against the Second Amendment. Still, in keeping with its principle of an individual's right to keep and bear arms, this new legislation may not infringe upon the stipulation in that document. According to the speech, a non-violent citizen with no criminal record may own a gun; he just won't be able to store it at home. It must be in a secure, guarded location. Diabolical! And it stinks, I know. But it doesn't surprise me."

"What about hunters? What about home defense, Dylan? You've got a few guns at your ranch for varmints. Both the four-legged and two-legged kind."

"Yeah," Bob said. "When seconds count, the police are only minutes away."

"I'm sure they'll have some provision for that. They'll have to."

After a few more miles of driving, Bob's phone rang again.

"Hey, Robert dear, I was thinking. You can't come back here right? Why don't you check out our new digs? Maybe take a little side trip to the Rockies?"

After switching drivers, attempting to stay off major freeways, traveling night and day, the trio scoped out a rundown used car lot on the outskirts of Alamosa, in southern Colorado.

"Alright, Bob, you've still got the I.D. I made up for you in Texas, right?"

"Yeah, but I'll never get used to people calling me by my new name. That's for sure."

"Well you better! That's for double sure. Unless you want to be the first-class ticket for some federal prosecutor launching his career into the national spotlight. They run about a 90% kill rate, you know, and it can cost over $200,000 to defend yourself. Besides, it's a good strong, yet unobtrusive name. Slips in and out of your mind easily."

"If you say so. Shouldn't we all go up to the property? What if it's a dump?"

"This is about the closest point for both of us to go our separate ways. Besides, didn't Julie say the woman sustained herself alone, year round?"

"Yeah, so?"

"Well if an eighty-seven-year-old woman can do it, I would think you can pick up where she left off."

"Yeah, Dad, Dylan's right. You can do it. Just get the place together and hide out until mom can get there. It's the best idea."

"He's right, Mr. R. It's just like we discussed, and we got you a good bunch of supplies. You shouldn't starve; you've got lanterns and cooking fuel, soap, bedding and clothes, fishing tackle. Everything on the list, not to mention what the old woman has lying around. You'll be fine. You just need a vehicle. I've already spotted a pretty decent looking 4x4 truck with a camper shell in the lot. I'll go snag it. We transfer your stuff over, and you should make it almost all the three hundred miles with one fill up."

"I'll do it at night, as usual. With hat and shades," Bob sighed.

"For real, Dad. Your picture is still splashing across the news nationwide. But it's amazing how different you look without your beard."

"Yeah, and it helps that they think you're dead also, Mr. R. That's for sure."

*****

With a reconditioned mountain capable truck, directions interpreted from the attorney's letter and Julie's memory, Bob was ready to set out to the mountain property left by Julie's benefactor. Judging from Julie's description of the keys included with the deed transfer papers, and a messaged smartphone photo, all he needed was a pair of bolt cutters and some new locks to gain entry and then secure the property.

"Bye, Dad."

"So long, Mr. Revere, it's been real. Remember to minimize your trips to the store. Stay as close to zero exposure as you can 'till this thing becomes a distant memory. That solar charger should keep your phone going for quite a while if the generator goes out. And we shouldn't have any problems with my strip-script software."

"Yeah, if there are any problems, just call and tell me."

"Very funny, Mr. R., or should I say, Mr. Nelson. Good luck with your new-fangled life. It looks like things are going to work out."

"Yeah, new life . . . You know what they say—the secret to living a good life is not to be too afraid of death," he said with a smile.

"I never heard that before. Did you just make that up?"

"Neither have I, Dad," Brandon added.

"Sure did. Appropriate too."

"Huh?"

"It was made up by a dead man."

As Dylan and Brandon proceeded back to the ranch in Texas, they monitored the news and checked the ATF website. For firearm enthusiasts, it was a nightmare. A new Executive Order, a national firearms mandate, was signed into law. Talking heads on all the news shows had a field day. Both sides of the argument were aired, however it soon became apparent that the corporate media was carrying the torch of the state. Reports favoring the strict new gun ordinance outpaced those against by eight to one. To those who still could think, it was obvious the media was propagating a national neutering of the citizens.

Everyone was aware of the consequences of non-compliance. Ex-lovers would turn in each other if they suspected illegal activity or possession of guns. Divorced women would rat out their former husbands to collect the $1,000 per gun reward. Neighbors would be suspicious of neighbors. Friends and family members were warned not to hide weapons or ammunition of die-hard 'over my dead body' types.

It was stipulated that people living remotely, far away in the back woods, with wolves, bears, or other life-threatening wild animals could maintain a weapon at home after passing a background check, a medical and psychological exam, a safety course, proven proficiency with the weapon, and a two-year license review. If they moved to town, the privilege was revoked, and guns would be stored as stipulated under the new law.

Those involved in security guarding VIPs, cash, jewels, or other high value items could also obtain permits. Only those living more than fifteen minutes from worst-case police response, with an active restraining order on a known abusive individual, could keep a weapon at home. Types of guns, modifications, lengths of barrels, types of ammunition and caliber, ages of those allowed a permit to possess, were all redefined. Military-style weapons, the favorite of many former gun-owners, were now illegal.

Guns and ammunition relinquished to the government were compensated by giving the donor tax credits, EBT food stamps, or monetarily reimbursement by a margin of .785 of the firearm's assessed value. The small percentage of persons allowed to keep a gun were issued ammunition micro-stamped on both the outside and inside of the casing, as mandated by the new law. All bullets, shotgun shells, and casings could now be traced to the person they were issued to. Licensing of these individuals was required every two years, with mandatory inspection of the weapon as a condition of licensing. Ammunition was accounted for and unused ammo had to be on hand, or returned to the storage facility. Reloading, possession of unregistered ammunition, reloading supplies or equipment, was now illegal.

Hunting was allowed in a severely controlled and restricted manner. Once the hunters passed a background check, a mental and physical exam, completed a safety course and paid for tags, they were allowed to check out their guns after signing paperwork defining the location of the hunt and estimated time of return of the weapon and ammo to the approved storage facility.

Any variance in the sanctioned schedule was subject to fines, loss of gun ownership for life, imprisonment, or any combination of these penalties. Hunters were required to carry a smartphone or other GPS enabled device at all times and sign a release that they could be stopped and searched without cause. Detachable magazines were outlawed, as were assault rifles and military-style rifles. The justification being, if a person wasn't in the military, why would they need an assault rifle!

Gun ranges were tightly controlled. Persons could shoot the guns they had stored there. The weapon could only be transported to another range with an approved permit. Again, any variance of the transport permit conditions was subject to severe penalties.

Any modifications of firearms had to be done at a government-sanctioned facility. All aspects of gun ownership now carried a fee—transport permits, licensing, storage, maintenance and modifications. Checking out your gun to hunt. Buying or selling a weapon, medical and psychological exams, and inspections of home or business property was an agreement every registered gun owner signed.

Shooting on private property, unless approved, licensed, and registered as hunting, was now illegal. The reason spewed by the obedient newscasters parroting Washington was if target practice occurred under conditions not surveyed and controlled by the government, it could lead to the terrorist training of an opposition force.

In short, the government had sucked the fun out of hunting, marksmanship competition and target shooting like minnows caught in a whirlpool. The deep state—those that really controlled everything—were now true masters over their domain.

FIFTY

Julie and Susan were waiting on the porch when Brandon and Dylan pulled up to the main house. The road-weary college roommates were happy to be home, even more so now, being showered with hugs and kisses and great delight at their return.

"He should be fine, Mom. Dylan scored him a used truck in good shape, and we set him up with plenty of supplies."

"Yes, but your father knows nothing about raising chickens, milking cows, or running a farm."

"He'll learn. I've been doing it since I was a little girl. Most of what to do, you already know. You just don't know you know it . . . You know?"

All eyes turned to Susan. "Little sister, that was the best homecoming thing I could have heard. We're sure glad to be back." A big smile lit across his face as Dylan hugged his sister.

*****

Dylan and Brandon, having missed the enrollment date for the fall semester, spent a lot of time reviewing the website. "Look here," Brandon said. "It seems many people who were commenting and leaving posts have been receiving notices to turn in any unregistered weapons. They're reporting it's only those who actually went to the site or looked it up on their smart phone. People that never went online to check it out were notified with letters later on."

"I believe it," said Dylan. "Keywords on smart devices like stash, hide, keep, store, hold-on-to, can peg you as someone asking a buddy to hide a gun. Same as if you're a member of some political crowd, donor to a First or Second Amendment group, gun association, or other quasi-antiestablishment organization. You are marked as a sympathizer. It looks like the full control of the smart device infected world has been turned inward.

"These days there are millions of cell phone zombies that've been brainwashed into submission. With facial recognition and psy-op algorithms, they can read your expression when you are watching a video, newscast, or anything on your screen. If you display a worried look when they air a show about gun owners going to jail, it's flagged and you end up on a list of people they might pay a midnight visit to. It's written in your phone contract that continuing the conversation means you've given your consent."

"And don't forget spy-patents issued for big data. Heart rate steering wheel sensors, other monitors detecting radio volume, conversations with certain pitch, or tone of voice indicating fatigue, or if you've been drinking, or talking on your cell phone are all scooped up and sold to your insurance company. And not just driving insurance—health as well.

"Check this out, dude. You know those robotic vacuum cleaners that scurry around your house? They work by mapping the area so they don't miss anything. Some models send that information to their corporate headquarters. They say it's so they can assist other smart devices in your wireless home system. How about the government getting a hold of that intel? Say they targeted you? They'd know right where your bed was. Right where to send the missile or SWAT team. It's downright spooky."

"I remember what a tech guy told me once," said Brandon. "He said there are many Big Brothers out there. When a software company gives you something for free, they put a tail on you and sell your profile. All of a sudden you become the product."

"You'll recall what happened during World War Two. The government locked up more than 100,000 U.S. citizens because they happened to be Japanese.

Remember it's not: are you paranoid? It's: are you paranoid enough!"

"I hear ya, bro. It's like what Einstein said. What we heard in Poli-Sci class, 'Unthinking respect for authority is the greatest enemy of truth.'"

"Yeah, or else it's: 'Attempt to correct or educate a fool, and he will hate you. Enlighten a wise man, and he will thank you.' These days we've privatized the ugliest act of government—war. If war wasn't profitable, do you think the elites would advocate for it?"

"How about this, I've seen on the news where they've confiscated guns from little old ladies in the ghetto and given them pepper spray, or stun guns. They called it forced re-accommodation. That's way beyond homeland security prohibiting facial cream or toothpaste on airplanes. What a joke! We're the ancient Romans on steroids, with satellite tracking, scud missiles, laser-guided smart bombs, biological weapons, cyber warfare, the works. Are you going to trust the people that told you Iraq had weapons of mass destruction? When the empire turns in on itself, as all dying empires do—and we don't have guns to protect ourselves—we're doomed."

"I know, but enough gloom and doom. What was that letter you received yesterday anyway?" Brandon said.

"It was a reply to an offer I sent out to sell my strip-script software to a high-tech company for fifty million dollars, probably about one-tenth its worth. Dude, they're interested, and judging by the letter I can probably squeeze 'em for forty million, at least. I'll have more than enough to throw you and Susan a great wedding."

"Wow cool. Way cool, Dylan, that's great. Hell, I thought it was pretty good when we found out the FBI was no longer monitoring the ranch. Said they had no concrete evidence anybody here was involved. Even though your website is registered to this address."

"It's under a fake name, but I was lucky they didn't want to push it. They were just happy Bob got killed in the explosion when he blew the bridge," Dylan said with a wink to Brandon.

FIFTY-ONE

❝ Hey, Pops, you can do me better than that. And hit me with some of those mashed potatoes too, will ya?"

"I guess that hole in your leg didn't fix itself while you were away at college did it, Jonah? You're stuffing your face like a starving lion," Jay said, while serving him up a plate of turkey.

"Well you know, all that hard studying sure can make a guy hungry. Say, Dad, tell me more about your last case. The guys in the dorm were wondering if you were going to be interviewed on TV. That's a hell of an assignment to be the last one before you retired. I guess you were sort of lucky that guy Bob Revere was blown up, along with the bridge, huh?"

With a stiff upper lip, retiring Agent Carver dished himself some stuffing while answering. "I guess you could say that, son. That's what they've been reporting for the last two weeks. It did wrap up the case nicely for this tired, old servant of the people."

"The guys and I have been following that group on The Anger Express website. A lot of people were."

"Yeah. Traffic was very high, especially conversations and posts about those terrorists."

"I know, Dad. Did you know there are more than one billion people on social media? That's one-seventh of the world's population."

Scooping up some green bean casserole, Jay replied, "That many, huh?"

"That's right. You remember a few years ago a major national bank wanted to put a five-dollar fee on people's checking accounts? It really struck a nerve with account holders. One woman started a social movement against it. Soon, so many people agreed with her that the bank reversed its policy in less than a month."

"Really?"

"That's right, dear," commented Annett Carver, Jay's wife. "I remember that. Aunt Jackie is with that bank. They're huge, one of the biggest in the country. I remember her telling me one-third of the customers said they were ready to switch banks, or go over to credit unions. It even shut down the bank's website. People were letting their fingers do the squawking."

"Yeah, Mom, that's the power of social media. That's how the Arab Spring got going, people posting and texting to meet in the town square and demonstrate. I heard the governments in Egypt and other Middle Eastern countries shut down websites but they couldn't stop people with cell phones. Probably because that would shut down their own communication systems also."

"That was a clear message we got at the bureau, so many posts of people supporting that terrorist—or activist group as you like to call them. The government was threatened, along with the corporations and people on Wall Street. That's why they wanted us to slam a lid on it ASAP."

"I don't know, Dad, as far as what we saw, they just did stuff that could be bad. They never actually did anything bad. They didn't kill anybody or blow anything up. They even handed out turkeys to needy families in Sacramento. But somehow that story got all twisted around. Denied later as some sort of street fair. Plus a big part of it didn't make any sense. Why would a group like that suddenly blow up the Golden Gate Bridge? I don't get it. Neither do a lot of the guys in the dorm. They wonder if the government just conveniently blamed the activists and started this crazy gun confiscation thing."

Jay poured some gravy on his mashed potatoes. Stirring it around a bit more than necessary, he said, "I don't know, son. I'm inclined to agree, but I just don't know. "

"What are you going to do now, Dad, with all your free time?"

After serving himself a nice slice of turkey, he looked to his wife. "Actually, Annett, I was thinking about going for a little drive, see some of the country. Mike and I have been talking about it for a while."

Annett turned to Jay. "It's nice you're finally telling me."

"I wasn't going to just disappear. We're thinking of doing some traveling, maybe you and I end up moving out of this god-awful heat hole. Somewhere up in the mountains maybe."

"Really, when do you plan on going? And what about me?"

"In a few months. I've got more than one hundred days of comp-time saved up in twenty years of service with no vacations or sick days. I've got some stuff to do around here first. We figure we'll go after the winter storm season but before you retire from the school district. We'll be looking for a small cabin or house by a lake."

"That does sound charming, Jay. I wouldn't mind living in the country, as long as it isn't too far from shopping."

Jay scooped some cranberry and turkey onto a buttered roll, placed another roll on top of it, making a mini sandwich, and took a bite. "Don't worry, dear, I did say house or cabin, not cave or tent."

FIFTY-TWO

Almost four months later:

As the time passed, Julie continued her three-day-a-week appointments with the health study. In reverse course of her becoming sick, she no longer needed a wheelchair, abandoned her walker, put away her cane, and eventually could walk without assistance. Sensation and control returned to her legs and feet, while sparkle returned to her eyes. Although she had never lost all her sparkle, being the kind of woman she was.

It was never determined if the study and medicine regimen involving Invigratol was extended due to the appeals of some radical group angling for dramatic social change. However, it was no secret the scientists, medical practitioners, and visiting 'suits' were quite pleased that the enrollees all reported diminished appetite and lost weight during the course of the study. The reversal of the debilitating effects of ALS were considered a positive result, although minor, in comparison.

"You sure you don't want me to go with you, Mom? It's about 900 miles you know— give or take. I could fly back, no problem."

"That's alright, honey. It's been awhile since I've taken a long drive by myself. It'll give me a chance to clear my head. Get over being on the path to death, that sort of thing,"

"It's good you're driving, Mrs. R. It's harder for them to track you than if you took a plane or a train. That is, if they're still following us, of course."

"Oh, Dylan, it's been months. Don't you think if they really wanted us they would have done something by now?"

"You never can be too careful."

"You're paranoid."

Dylan looked at Brandon and said, "I guess she doesn't know the saying, does she?"

"I guess not."

"Oh, will you two stop it! I just want to forget the whole thing. Uncle Joe, the FBI, the whole thing," said Susan. "I'm just glad we're alright, and Julie is well on the way to being completely cured. That's all."

"I'm glad too. You're sure you got all your stuff, Mom?"

"I'm sure. I don't need much to drive to see your father. Some clothes, personal items, that sort of thing. It does concern me that we haven't heard from him in a while. What's it been, more than two weeks now?"

"Sixteen days," said Dylan. "I've tried everything I can with the cell phone I set up for him. I sure hope he's all right. I hope the FBI really did drop the case, unable, as they said, to link my website, or those dynamite boxes, to any of us."

"I hear ya, bro," said Brandon. "And we sure as hell dodged a bullet when they thought he was killed blowing up the Golden Gate Bridge."

Julie shifted back and forth on her feet. She scraped a small arc in the sand with the toe of her sandal while standing by her car. She gave a long hug to Susan first, and then Dylan. "You both have been so wonderful. I just can't thank you enough." She opened the door, got inside, and rolled the window down. "I guess there's only one way to find out. Someone's going to have to go check on your father." She lowered a pair of sunglasses from her brow to shield against the noonday sun. "I'll call you as soon as I know something."

"Bye Mom, I love you."

"Drive safe, Mrs. R.," said Dylan.

"Y'all come back when you get a chance," said Susan.

Julie smiled at the trio. She grasped Susan's hand and said, "I sure will." She gave a short wave to the others, and proceeded down the long driveway toward the open road.

FIFTY-THREE

A s he told his wife, after getting caught up around the house with a few please-honey-dos, Rufus J. Carver planned a long drive early in his retirement. He longed for a cool place in the Rocky Mountains, should something available catch his eye.

Carver and his retired buddy, Michael Washington, were taking their time hitting most of the appealing golf courses along the way. Michael had a special pass allowing them a discount at many hotels and ten to fifteen percent off on meals. It also allowed for reduced entry fees to many National Parks. Rufus told his wife he didn't know when they'd be back. He said that he was going to enjoy a well-deserved vacation after more than twenty years with the bureau. Besides golf, the two travelers planned to do some fishing. She was happy to have him out of the house for a while.

*****

Bob was busy loading hay into the cow's feeding trough as Julie emerged from the chicken coop with a basket of fresh eggs. Neither of them heard the sound of car doors shutting on the dirt road down by the overgrown fence to their property.

"I'll have to see if we can trade some of these eggs for something else we need. Maybe a new cell phone charger since you lost yours at the river before I made it up here."

"No kidding," Bob said. "I never thought a few chickens could produce so many eggs."

"Must be a pretty prolific rooster," Julie said, with a long look at her husband in his tight-fitting, well-worn jeans, and open shirt with the sleeves rolled up. "It suddenly occurs to me I don't have any plans for after dinner. Maybe I could wrangle myself a handsome ranch hand to ease some of the tension linked with running this place," she said with a smile.

"Well I don't know. What do you plan on feeding that handsome ranch hand for dinner?"

"I'm making a chicken pot pie in the Dutch oven. If you're nice, I may do a berry cobbler for dessert."

"Will that be before or after certain tension-easing procedures?"

"I don't know. I imagine that depends on the ranch hand."

Bob took Julie in his arms and gave her a long, loving, kiss.

*****

"I'd say you're doing pretty well for a dead man."

The romantic embrace was interrupted as the surprised couple spun around to see two older black men wearing casual sports clothes ambling up the dirt road toward the ranch compound.

"Agent Carver, how nice to see you . . . I think."

"You're looking good yourself, Mrs. Revere. I understand you completed a drug study course for Invigratol. Seems as though it helped your condition very much. I'm glad it worked out for you."

Bob shot a quick glance toward the ranch house. Then another at the beltline of Agent Carver. If he had a gun concealed under the loose-fitting Hawaiian shirt, Bob was unable to detect it. He could make it to the dwelling or to the woods, but there was something in the man's off-the-cuff manner that told him he didn't have to run.

"Agent Carver. I've heard about you."

"And I've come to know quite a bit about you as well, Mr. Revere. In fact you're the most notorious unsolved case of my career."

"Come again?"

"Although on extended vacation at this time, I am still an agent of the FBI. Got a gun and handcuffs right here to prove it." Carver lifted his shirt revealing the pistol stuffed in his waistband as he pulled a pair of handcuffs out from behind his belt. He took a couple of steps toward Bob while casually preparing the handcuffs to be placed on his suspect.

Bob's mind raced. He considered tackling the older black man, throwing him to the ground, and taking his weapon. Yet he didn't move.

"What time is it, Michael?" Carver said, throwing a glance toward his companion.

With a look of bewilderment, Washington answered, "Six-thirty. It's six-thirty, Jay. What are you doing? I thought you were retired."

"I'm near retirement, but no, technically I'm still a legitimate agent. Obliged to bring in lawless suspects in any case assigned to me—dead or alive."

Carver, standing within arm's reach of Bob, still holding the handcuffs, was rubbing his chin with his other hand while ignoring the others and looking at the sunset. "Let me see. I figure it's roughly about an hour's drive to get out of these twisted mountain roads, and onto a main highway. It's about another three and a half hours to Denver, the closest FBI branch in this region. That's four and a half hours.

"Plus, I'm getting hungry. We'll need to stop for dinner. That'll take an hour easy. By my calculations, that adds up to five and a half hours. We'd be getting to the Federal Building right around midnight. Unless there's traffic, road closures, detours, hell . . . it could take more than an hour for dinner. Especially if we enjoyed a couple of cocktails before our meal. Either way, we'd be hard pressed to make it by twelve P.M. wouldn't we?"

His traveling companion answered with furrowed eyebrows in a slow voice, "Yeah. I guess that's right."

"Well," Carver said, now looking at Bob while turning the handcuffs over in his hand, "That's it then."

Julie spoke up, "What do you mean, that's it?"

"That's it! Not enough time! My formal retirement starts tomorrow . . . at twelve o'clock midnight. To-day is my last day as an official FBI agent. And I'll tell you, after arresting bad guys for some twenty-plus years, I sure as hell am not going to be doing any of that heroic citizen's arrest crap anytime soon."

The bulging artery in Bob's neck started to sub-side, along with his rapid breathing. His facial expression eased from tangled thoughts of grabbing guns, pushing people to the ground and taking off, to shaking his head and considering these new arrivals in a different light.

Julie, squinting her eyes while relaxing her face in-to a sly smile looked at Carver and said, "You're mean."

Carver, now smiling himself, addressed the cou-ple. "Oh, don't worry. The case is closed. As soon as the bridge was blown and the national news spread the story that you and your group were domestic terrorists set on forceful revolution, I knew something was wrong. My son convinced me that your little escapades were too non-violent to be really dangerous and radical. Plus, I saw who was driving the rig just before the bridge was destroyed. Too bad about your RV. Obviously it was part of the plan to pin the whole thing on you."

Julie stood silent as Bob answered, "You saw the driver?"

"That's right! And it wasn't you."

"Really! I mean, I know. Who was it then?"

"I don't know. It looked like someone of Mediterranean descent. That's all I can say. My partner was calling for backup and didn't see him but I know for sure it wasn't you."

"Good of you to say so, Agent . . . I mean, soon-to-be citizen, Carver."

"Oh, hold on a sec, I'm so rude. This is Michael Washington, my longtime friend, golf, and fishing buddy."

"Pleased to meet you both," said Michael. I've heard a lot about you."

"I'll bet you have," Julie chimed in. "So if you're not here to arrest anybody, why are you here?"

"I didn't say I wasn't here to arrest anybody."

Bob tensed as he took a half step toward the shortest path to the woods.

"Just kidding," Jay said with a wide grin. "You can stay dead, Bob. I'm sure the big boys pulling the strings would be quite embarrassed if you popped up out of nowhere now so many months after they've been hanging the whole thing on you via every TV station from here to Abu Dhabi. Plus, I found out my former tech-savvy partner has been reassigned."

"So, why are you here then, Mr. Carver?" Julie said.

"Just out taking a little drive in the woods. Looking for a place for the wife and me to settle down. That, and I never like to leave a case unsolved."

"Bob—everyone, I'm getting tired of standing here with these eggs. Why don't we all go inside? Shall we?"

Bob couldn't help stealing another glance at slight bulge at the bottom of the colorful flowered shirt worn by his uninvited guest before saying, "Yeah, okay, I guess so. Let's all go inside."

*****

Julie brought out some iced tea as the men sat in the living room of the small ranch house.

"I like your place here," Jay said.

"Looks like good fishing around here too," his friend Michael stated.

"Bob and I do pretty well down at the small river running through the property. But tell me, I've been wondering all this time, how did you find us?"

Jay smiled. "I was the senior FBI agent assigned to your case, you know! I didn't do twenty-plus years chasing bad guys without learning a thing or two."

Bob and Julie exchanged glances.

"Oh, I'm sorry. Please forgive me. I didn't mean you. A bad guy never offered me a cold glass of iced tea. This is wonderful, Julie, if I may call you that."

"You may. Everybody else does."

"To continue, as I'm sure you might guess, we monitored all of your communications 24/7. We even have a special department dealing solely with the U.S. mail. If Santa Claus sent you a letter lick-sealed by a reindeer, we could open it, read it, and send it on to you so that you would never know it had been tampered with. All that and we'd still get the DNA to identify the reindeer as an added bonus."

"Makes sense," Bob said.

"We checked out this place as soon as we discovered it was left to you, figured the lady must have told you in advance of the legal notice sent to you, but you and your gang were nowhere to be found, so we kept looking elsewhere."

"So now you're here looking for tips on the local fishing holes?" Bob said with a cynical inflection over the top of his glass as he took a sip.

"Something like that. That, and I don't like to leave any case unresolved. Like I said, I am one tenacious son of a bitch. In my mind we can put this one to rest. I always figured you'd end up here. I know I would—case closed. There is one thing that bothers me though."

"Go on," Bob said.

"How did you and your little band of—what would my son call you—activists, talk to each other? We figured you were using burner phones. But when we traced all the unregistered traffic for pay-as-you-go phones, we got nothing."

"Remember when you came to the ranch in Texas and met Dylan? He developed something he called strip-script. It camouflages any signal and destroys any text after its read. He sold it for millions, and is planning a trip to Europe to tour the continent."

"You don't say. Well, I want to thank you for the tea, both of you. And I might also add that, Bob, if I can call you that—yours is the best case I never got an official collar out of. I'm proud to have been a part of it. I know now why you did what you did, and I heartily agree. This country is messed up politically, from the inside out. And although we never could prove that your son and his Texas friend, Dylan, were involved, even though it was mighty suspicious how all your stunts appeared the next day on his website, I'm glad it turned out the way it did. I'll tell you something else, too. When we intercepted cell texts from the San Francisco area, the day of the disaster, we got a couple associated with something called operation one-double-x-31.

"Yeah, okay."

"It didn't take the crypto-boys long to decipher it. Seems it comes out in Roman numerals to mean a one, and two xs, and three ones. In other words 1X--which is nine, X1—which is eleven, followed by 11—which is two. In other words... 9-11 2.0, just as they are spewing it on all channels. The first thing you learn in this business is there's no such thing as a coincidence. The job was a set-up, with you as the fall guy.

"Their master plan was rolled out real soon after killing hundreds and destroying a world class landmark. My son discussed it in his class regarding constitutional amendments. He wrote a paper on it. Well, we better be going. Come on, Michael, we'll show ourselves out."

They all stood as Jay and his friend turned to leave. "By the way, where would there be some good fishing spots around here anyway?" Michael asked.

"You go back down the road about five miles or so until you see a large dome of granite on your right. You'll cross a bridge. Don't worry, it shouldn't blow up. Park there and hike down, it's not very far. The river widens out and you'll see some of the best pools to drown a worm in that you can find in this part of the valley," Bob said.

"I may move to the Rockies. I've been telling the wife I want to move to the mountains."

"There are a few nice places for sale. And if you do move up here, come on back. We've got plenty of eggs," Julie said.

Bob and Jay shook hands, nodding, giving each other a long eyeball-to-eyeball look, with a thin smile. Both men knowing they could never see each other again.

FIFTY-FOUR

The engines revved and the 'fasten seatbelts' sign came on as the stewardess announced for all passengers to switch off any electronic devices. Dylan was reviewing the news feed on his cell phone and was slow to comply. The 747 taxied down the runway approaching its position for takeoff. She continued explaining how to duck in an emergency and how the seat cushions could be used as life preservers should the trans-Atlantic flight be forced into the water.

Walking down the aisle, she stopped by his seat. "Sir, you'll have to shut off your phone before takeoff. It's a safety precaution."

"Uh, okay. I was just looking at this story about how the Golden Gate Bridge was destroyed. They're saying a radical group of terrorists did it. Actually, there was another rather obscure story out of Sacramento that the same group was giving out turkeys to the homeless the day before. They couldn't have done it. The story is a blatant lie!"

"That may very well be, sir, but I still have to ask you to put your phone away for takeoff. It's an FAA requirement."

"Yeah, I know." Dylan switched off his device, wondering what the American people would do. Would they put the pieces together? Would they see this was another false flag event fostered by the globalists to further restrict basic freedom? Would they understand this as another action done by power-hungry parasites desiring nothing less than total planetary control?

As the attractive flight attendant leaned in close adjusting his seatbelt, she gave him a warm smile. "By the way, my husband agrees with you. He's a constitutional attorney. He's circulating a petition that will go before Congress to investigate the event. But between you and me, he wonders if it will gain any traction. He doubts the American people will stand up to a slowly encroaching tyranny. He sees them as too complacent, too unaware of the warnings of the founding fathers. He sees the frog dying in the pot."

Dylan knew about the frog-in-the-pot political theory. How a frog dropped into a pot of boiling water jumps out right away. But if the temperature is raised slowly around the hapless amphibian, he adjusts until he dies.

He leaned back in his seat thinking about what the insightful stewardess said about the warning of the founding fathers regarding a corrupt cavity-searching police-state government and how long the population would accept this Orwellian suppression.

As the plane left the runway, an advertisement came across the viewing screen on the back of the seat in front of him. Physbon Pharmaceuticals was announcing a forthcoming wonder drug to help curb the obesity epidemic sweeping the country.

Dylan wondered if his covert actions to point a finger at corporate/governmental collusion, along with his website, The Anger Express, might poke an open wound, thereby stimulating a nerve in the American people. He guessed the oligarchy hadn't gotten sufficient impact since a mass shooting from the thirty-second floor of a Las Vegas hotel into a crowd of country music fans. That's why they blew the Golden Gate. In a display of just how unorganized the whole affair was, there were many troubling elements reported by the lame-stream media itself.

Why would someone cart twelve to twenty rifles—reports varied—into a high-rise hotel unless to ultimately have them found thereby making a statement about too many guns? A person can only shoot one at a time! Also casinos, and their adjoining hotels, are some of the most heavily surveilled buildings in existence. Where was the camera footage of a single man humping multiple long bags or boxes to his room? And why was hotel staff not suspicious? Not to mention, how often does one hear about a happy, well-adjusted millionaire, who owns two airplanes, go off the rails and start shooting people? Why were two windows broken out, where as one with a clear line-of-sight would do? Of course, the purported lone gunman would never be questioned since being conveniently found dead at the scene.

There were several more highly doubtful points that could be found online, such as forensic acoustical evidence, and video of a second shooter. Doctors also reported wounds inconsistent with the type of weapon used. Alleged 'actors' hired to appear shot were rapidly recovering—and laughing in hospital beds, and the FBI wiped clean all of the concert-goers cellphones. The more he considered it, he figured they had botched that gun-control scare tactic with insufficient destruction of property, low body count, and poorly articulated press releases.

He laid his head back, closed his eyes and thought about what happened in Nazi Germany. He had to admit to himself—along with the pretty flight attendant's husband—he seriously wondered. Would the American people come together? He knew there were enough resources, technology, and brains on earth to satisfy man's need—but, as of yet—not his greed. He recalled a poem by an eighteenth-century, Oxford-educated English romantic poet he had come across some time ago: 'Rise like Lions after slumber, in unvanquishable number. Shake your chains to earth like dew, which in sleep had fallen on you—ye are many; they are few.'

THE END

For the record, I am not unsympathetic to the mass shootings (a term unofficially defined as a shooting with five or more victims — not necessarily deaths) that have become all too frequent in the United States. It's quite the opposite, in fact.

The reasons for these tragedies, if they are to be understood, stem from man's innate predisposition to violence, fueled by video games, movies, glorification of military conquest, poverty/despair and substandard mental health care — to name but a few. Those of religious background could easily make a case for pure evil. A study of cause-and-effect would fill many volumes yet we would still have the random, unpredictable event. Debate on this subject is beyond the scope of this composition.

In publishing this work of fiction, it is simply my intention to enlighten the public that you can't believe everything you see and hear. Huge lies have been propagated by our government on the nightly news to further Wall Street's and Washington's insatiable greed. Think about it: the prolonged wars, the bank bailouts, the medical care debacles, the tax giveaways to the exceedingly wealthy (including large corporations), safety net cutbacks, etc. — who benefits? Always the wealthy.

In closing, I will state that I do believe some form of restriction should be placed on weapons solely designed to kill massive numbers of people in the shortest amount of time possible. The general public does not have access to grenades, rocket launchers or tanks. Perhaps military-grade, semi-automatic rifles should be moved closer to this category. That said, perhaps a serious review of landmines, chemical/biological/nuclear, drones, and space-based military weapons is in order as well. Some would argue that this is not defense — it is offense!

There is evidence, however, that when an initial law is passed, it opens the gate for additional regulations and restrictions that can ultimately squash personal freedoms leading to an Orwellian scenario. Remember: making guns illegal to quell street violence is like making spoons illegal to defeat obesity. It is my belief that oppressive gun laws would be as effective as drug laws. Those prone to certain tendencies will do as they wish regardless of the consequences. Education and a restructuring of society may be a good start.

ABOUT THE AUTHOR

Educated at SJSU and Stanford University, Richard Lake is an award-winning author with more than a dozen articles on social commentary, read by over 250,000 people.

As a student of past and current geo-political trends, he focuses on what could be a horrific beginning to Act 3 for the United States of America.

ACKNOWLEDGEMENTS

I would like to thank the members of the Valley Writers Group. Without their direction, insight and patience—this book would not have been possible.

I also wish to acknowledge the support of my loving family, which has served as inspiration for this story.

Please write an Amazon review.
We're saving the world one book
at a time:
Contact author: lagomarsinorich@gmail.com

Made in the USA
San Bernardino, CA
15 February 2020